WHERE THE WEIRD

THINGS ARE

VOLUME 2

Edited by Austin P. Sheehan and
Clare Rhoden

First published by Deadset Press in 2023.

Cover design Copyright © Austin P. Sheehan.

Edited by Austin P. Sheehan and Clare E. Rhoden.

Acknowledgement of Country:

In the spirit of reconciliation, Deadset Press acknowledges the Traditional Custodians of country throughout Australia and their connections to land, sea and community. We pay our respect to their Elders past and present and extend that respect to all Aboriginal and Torres Strait Islander peoples today.

Acknowledgements:

This anthology was put together by a wonderful team of passionate writers, editors and readers that are spread all over Australia. Thank you to Clare Rhoden, Mikhaeyla Kopievsky, Maddie Jensen, and S. M. Isaac. Thank also go out to all the contributing authors, and to all those in the Australian Speculative Fiction community who submitted a story. The biggest thanks, however, must go to you, the reader. It is those who are willing to read, learn and share which allow myths and legends to live.

— Austin P. Sheehan, on behalf of Deadset Press.

CONTENTS:

Lake Charm is a tiny town nestled on the banks of the ancient Murray River, and is so quiet that ghosts go there to die.

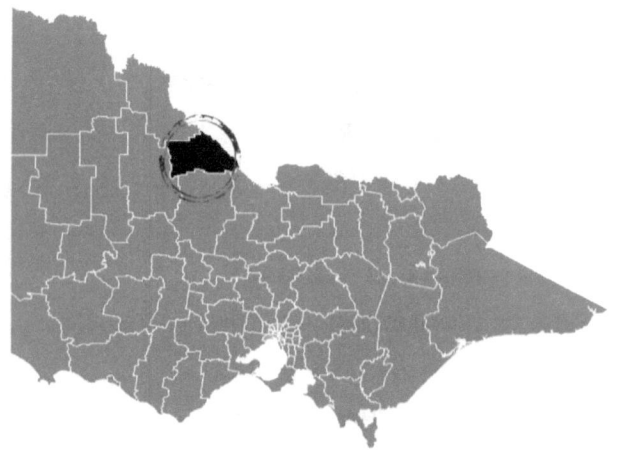

THE BOWL

Rue Karney

The Lake Charm Skate Bowl was a beauty, said to be the last of its kind in the country. The tooth fence around it, that was one of a kind, too. Rumour was that skaters from years past had stacked the thousands of incisors, canines and molars around the bowl to scare off pretenders.

Juke was no pretender. And the Lake Charm Bowl satisfied his cravings for those places that were all dried up; nothing but hollow husks and bones with no more juice to offer. Ever since he was a wriggling kid jumping off the roof of the backyard shed and pounding his bike over rough-made jumps, the hard places no one else wanted to be were where he was most at home. His van was stocked with water supplies and enough roo jerky, two-minute noodles, nuts and dried fruit to see him through the smoke-grey winter. When the bowl came into view he pulled off the highway, drove down the dirt road and parked inside the tooth fence.

Day one he got to work cleaning up the mess of splintered decks, rusted trucks, broken bottles and other crap that gathered in the bowl's base. The tattoos on his wiry biceps—frangipani on the left, snake on the right—slid over his muscles while he swept the bowl with a broom he fashioned from dry saltbush and string. Day two he scrounged supplies from a nearby dump and carried tins of paint, a couple of old paint rollers and a not too cracked tray from his van to the bowl. The winter sun bore down on his back as he touched up patches of bare concrete on the bowl with blue paint. Sweat beaded along his winged shoulder blades. It dribbled from under his arms, down his ribs and across the flat of his lean torso. Where he could he left the graffiti untouched out of respect for skaters long gone.

On the cold, dull morning of the third day he slid open the door of his van, sat on the step and stared into the scrubby landscape littered with wizened, old-men trees. He picked at food scraps between his teeth with a stick he'd whittled to a needle point then rubbed them with charcoal. He swirled water in his mouth and spat it onto the ground. His spittle frothed and disappeared into the dirt.

With toothpick in hand, he wandered over to check out his handiwork. The morning frost bit his skin. He stepped on the weed patches scattered across the dirt and cracked the ice with the soles of his feet. From the bowl's edge, he stared down at the three skater ghosts huddling in the shadows. He threw the toothpick into the bowl. The tallest ghost, shaved head and scarecrow lean, picked it up and poked it into her bony jaw. It fell through her empty body and onto the ground. The other two, skinny ghost-boys in baggy pants and faded shirts, hooted hollow-air laughs as the toothpick disintegrated into ash.

The scrubbing, cleaning and general ruckus Juke made when sorting out a place usually got rid of any unwanted post-lifers and, in his experience, most ghosts liked to keep to their own. All across the Wamba Wamba lands, across the Mallee scrub and beyond, towns were full of them, wandering the streets, their grey faces fixed in expressions of grief after too many years of heat and drought had killed their townships along with them. They were a sorrowful lot but not dangerous.

Skater ghosts were a different breed. Reckless and obsessed, they gave no fucks in death, just as they had given none in life.

The ghosts stood arm in arm, staring up at Juke with retributive eyes. He scratched the scars he'd collected from his last encounter with a dead skater who could not let go of their living dream. The puckered, flaky scratches across his chest and stomach itched like prickly caterpillars. He returned to his van and grabbed his board. His spine prickled. He ground his teeth and turned around.

It was the tall one. Dull sky loomed through her hollow eyes and her mouth was a loose flap with gums the colour of drought-ravaged earth.

"A tooth." She spread grey fingers towards Juke's mouth. "It's the price of skating the bowl."

Juke brushed dust off his jeans. There were other places he could go to skate. Abandoned towns were plentiful all through the Mallee. Most still had structures from before the country had burnt and dried to a crisp that a skater could make good use of. Car parks.

3

Buildings with rails leading up multiple flights of steps. Empty swimming pools. Warehouses. Shopping centres. The old Lake Boga skate park, with its ramps and funboxes, was less than thirty ks away. Sections of it were still skateable.

Juke swiped the ghost's hand away. "No thanks," he said.

"One tooth is all it takes," the ghost bargained. "One tooth today and you can skate until the sun goes down."

Juke was particular about his teeth to the point one ex had claimed he was obsessive. As a teen his shiny, white-toothed smile had launched him into a brief career as a catalogue model. It was a strange, bright-lights anomaly in a life paved with dirt, rocks and wild places. He'd tolerated the work until he had saved enough to leave home. His parents were okay, neither too nasty nor too nice; they just weren't his kind of people. When he left they had put up no fuss.

"You choose the tooth. I add it to our collection." The ghost's head inclined towards the bowl. "We get out of your way and it's yours until the sun goes down."

Juke ran his tongue around the thirty-two teeth that filled his mouth. Strong, straight teeth. No fillings. A few chips here and there, that was all.

"You know this bowl's one of a kind," she said.

The morning sun slid above the horizon and shimmered across the bowl's lip. The ghost was right. Compared to this place, Lake Boga was little more than cracked concrete and dust.

A canine scratched Juke's tongue with its sharp edge.

"It's just a tooth," she said.

"A tooth is a lot," he said.

"Is it?" Her skull creaked to the side. A strip of grey flesh hung loose from her scalp. Her skeleton fingers pushed against his lips.

"Hey!" Juke jumped back, but his own fingers were in his mouth tugging at the canine. It slid out of his gum, smooth as a gliding eel, and fell into his cupped palm.

"Easy-peasy." Her laugh wheezed like an infection as she plucked the tooth from Juke's hand. "The bowl's all yours. Make it proud."

* * *

The rattling teeth tolled a dark tune as Juke ran towards the bowl, his board tucked under his arm. The ghost was true to her word, and she and her companions vanished, leaving the wide, smooth empty space just for him. He dropped into the bowl, disappearing into the movement, his mind blank. He was the board and muscle and bone and air tumbling and dropping. His tricks were magic. Each landing was a perfect thing, each grind sublime, every flip and spin a neat calculation.

Juke skated. Time drifted. In a washed-out sky, the sun moved in its arc from morning to afternoon to dusk. It was a glowing orange ball above the horizon when the skater ghosts reappeared in the bowl.

Juke stumbled and fell off his board.

"Fun day?" The tall ghost picked up Juke's board and handed it to him.

"Yep." Juke brushed off a film of concrete dust and grinned like an idiot.

"See you tomorrow, maybe," she said.

The baggy-pants boys sniggered.

"Maybe." Juke skated up and around the shallow side of the bowl. He reached for the lip. His body was absent. His mind reeled. He dropped, skated, grabbed again and hauled himself up. He sat on the edge of the bowl and pulled his legs to his chest. His scraped skin beaded blood. Below him, the ghosts were silver shadows in the falling dark spinning across the bowl, hooting and hollering. A hot, dry wind billowed under his t-shirt. The ghost voices shivered through his veins and raised the fine hairs on his skin.

Juke hurried towards his van and locked himself in. He opened his mouth and peered at the reflection on the polished aluminium of his camp stove. The naked gum was grey and when he poked his tongue into the gap left by his absent tooth, it was ice cold.

* * *

During the night's thick hours a film strip of dreams ran through Juke's head. Swollen-eyed lovers dragged themselves across his mattress. Absent friends spoke in ear-piercing alarm. Long-dead dogs whimpered and shoved their dry noses against his skin. His hands struggled to pluck the images out of his head and found their way instead to his mouth, his teeth, his gums. He woke into a cold

6

grey day, coated in sweat, his dreams as ingrained in his skin as his tattoos. He crawled out of his sleeping bag and gulped water, his missing tooth aching like a stolen memory.

* * *

Juke stepped out into a day bloated with clouds hoarding rain. Across the empty land the tooth fence gleamed with a dull sheen. Somewhere along its length his canine had locked itself into place, a piece of him now part of the tooth-fence puzzle.

"Mornin'." The tall ghost shimmered into sight. "Nice day for it."

"Yeah." Juke gestured to the north-west. "I'm keen to get onto the road, maybe check out Lake Boga today."

The ghost's smile reflected Juke's lie. "It's only a tooth."

"Nah."

"Make your mouth nice and even."

"Once was enough." Juke cleared the scratch clawing at his throat. "Could never top yesterday."

"Have you looked at the bowl this morning?" She drifted towards it.

Juke rubbed his eyes. He blinked and opened them wide. The bowl was bigger than he remembered—deeper and wider—and its surface shone with a translucent sheen.

"What did you do to it?"

"Nothing. It responds to good skating, that's all." Her hand on Juke's shoulder was a spider's sticky web.

7

Juke frowned. "You've put some glamour on it."

"I don't have magical powers. It is what it is. All it wants is another tooth."

Juke crouched to look at the bowl from a lower angle. It shimmered like the ocean. He shook his head and batted away thoughts that he was crazy, that he'd lost his mind and become the looney loner who couldn't tell the sun from a golden coin. He ran his tongue across his upper teeth.

"What if I don't want to give you another tooth?"

"No tooth. No skate. I can't make the rules any more simple than that," she said.

"Why do you get to make the rules anyway?"

"I don't. The bowl does." The ghost shrugged. "Try skating without giving me a tooth first and see how far you get."

Juke ran towards the bowl's lip and jumped on his board. The wheels slid out from under him. The board flipped into the air. He sprawled backwards, slamming onto the ground. The board landed beside him with a dull thud.

"What the fuck!" He stood and shook off the dust.

"You want to skate then give me a tooth," the ghost said.

Juke turned to walk away. His feet sank into ankle-deep bulldust. He stumbled forward. The ghost stood over him.

"Your teeth are pretty," she said. "The bowl likes that. *That's* the type of glamour it likes."

He dragged himself out of the bulldust and looked beyond the ghost to the glimmering bowl.

"A tooth is such a small, small price to pay," she said.

His fingers pushed into his mouth and pincered them around his second eye tooth. It slid out easy, no resistance.

She plucked it from between his thumb and index finger and closed it into her fist. "The bowl is yours."

Juke ran at the bowl and dropped off the lip. His heart soared. Light flowed through his veins and bones. Gravity could not bind him to the earth and when he did air there was only the sky, the bowl and his board. There was no sweat, no fatigue, no pain. He was pure, weightless. All energy and no fear.

As the light faded into sunset the three ghosts hovered at the edge of the bowl. Juke carved around it, heading towards them. The air thickened. His stomach plummeted but he did not deviate, and when the three spirits passed through him dread drenched his body in a chemical flood. His body connected with the earth, a sack of suffering cast down by a malevolent god.

Juke gasped for breath from empty lungs.

"Another perfect day," the tall ghost said. She hovered above Juke, flanked by her ghost boys. The trio stared down at him, their mouths spread in toothless grins.

Juke closed his eyes. The spectres invaded his vision. Eyes wide open or squeezed shut they were there looming, laughing, poking him with insubstantial fingers and toes. A relentless chill burned his skin. The ghosts mocked him with hollow voices that wormed in his ears. He opened his mouth to scream and woke up in his van naked, his skin slimy with sweat and dust, his mouth as crusty as the bottom of a cockatoo's cage.

He peeled himself from the sticky vinyl floor, flicked on his torch and shone it around. His sleeping bag was scrunched up in one corner of the van; in the other corner, his clothes were strewn like rags. Through the window of his van, the tooth fence glowed silver under the half moon, no stars. The black sky filled him with panic. He pinched himself until his skin reddened and picked at the scabs on his knees until they bled. He took a towel from the floor and wrapped it around his waist. When he opened the van's door, he swung the torch around to check for snakes before stepping barefoot onto the ground. Fire crackled in the distance, and with it came the acrid stench of burning rubber though no flames lit the sky. The skater ghosts' hollow chortles shivered through him. His testicles shrivelled. He went back to his van and did not sleep.

* * *

The road to the bowl had been long and short, straight and twisted, a legend and a fact. The twenty-four hours it took to drive there from the last place Juke had called home had taken a year of fossicking and scavenging, picking over the bones discarded by others too weak to endure.

Almost all the people he'd once known now belonged in two camps: those who chose to live under strict laws in the so-called climate-safe belts, and those who were dead. There was only one other who had taken to the road. Another skater, Moggo, who had headed south to the ocean. Juke liked it better away from the coast where there were fewer people fighting over the scraps of existence.

He didn't miss the company of humans. He did miss his dog. Every now and then, driving through a town, he'd pass by a skinny-ribbed mutt still eking out a feed. Once he'd even stopped and opened his door, thinking to take one in. The dog had bared its teeth and snapped. Juke had slammed his door shut.

* * *

Juke wiped the dust from the windscreen with the back of his left hand and turned the keys in the ignition. The engine rumbled.

The tall ghost slid in and sat on the empty passenger seat. "You seen the bowl today, right?"

Juke's hands sweated on the steering wheel. In front of him, the bowl shimmered under the morning sun. Behind him was the tooth fence, and the dirt road that led to the highway.

"You got some sick tricks and that's the truth. The air you got, we were most impressed," the tall ghost went on, "the best we've seen in a long time."

"I've had my fun," he said. He pressed his foot against the accelerator. The engine coughed then revved.

"Why you so attached to them teeth anyway? What else they gonna buy you?"

Juke opened his mouth to answer. His teeth vibrated in his gums. His jaw clicked shut.

"Just one more tooth. Just one more day," the ghost said.

Juke switched the engine off.

* * *

One more day became another and another and another until the sun rose one morning and his gums were almost bare.

"No more." Juke scraped a razor over his stubble. "Today, I leave." He opened his mouth and looked at his blurred reflection on the aluminium camp stove. His gums, smooth and grey all along, ended on each side with a wisdom tooth. The four of them shone, white and luminous. He ground them against each other. The sound they made was wheels on bitumen.

"Lucky last," the ghost said. She was a chill sitting on his shoulders.

"What do you mean?"

"Wisdom teeth are special, they're a package deal," she said.

"You're not getting these. I'm leaving today," Juke tapped the edge of his razor into the round, stainless-steel basin. Grey suds and short, thick dark hairs scummed the surface of the water. The ghost stuck her finger into the mucky bowl. It turned blue as the ocean. It swelled like a wave and spread out and up and around and Juke

12

was sitting in the bottom of it, his skateboard under his arm, a phalanx of ghosts surrounding him.

"It would be wise to hand over the teeth," the tall ghost said. She laughed at her dumb joke.

"No," he said.

"It's gonna happen. You might as well enjoy your last ride," she said.

Invisible hands prised open Juke's jaws. Bony fingers wrenched out the four wisdom teeth, one by one, and threw them against the bowl's shimmering surface.

The ghosts vanished. Juke's board dropped and rolled, and nudged his sneakered feet. He kicked, pushed and glided. He grinded and flipped; he skated and soared. His tricks shamed past rivals, outshone his old-school heroes, and obliterated the championship medal right off that smart-arse punk who'd hung it around his bony chest, courtesy of a famous last name.

Juke spun in the air until the bowl below him blurred into the blue sky above and his mind narrowed into a singular, focused thought.

If there's a right way to die, this has gotta be it.

* * *

Juke woke up at the bottom of the bowl, staring into a black sky. His flesh was ice gripping his rattling bones. From somewhere close a fire crackled, and an orchestra of rubbing insect sounds scritched inside his head. His absent teeth hummed inside his mouth that opened up, lips loose and flapping, gums smooth as the bowl's surface. He stood on his board. The concrete surface below him fell away, and he was weightless, walking on air, on nothing at all. He floated above the earth towards the tooth fence that shone like the moon.

A slice of silver rippled across the sky, a tear in the night's curtain. Juke fell among dozens of skater ghosts, all standing around a fire that burned indigo and grey.

The tall ghost drifted towards Juke and grinned her toothless grin. She patted Juke's shoulder with chilled air fingers. "Now it's time to party with us."

Juke gave in to the slow drift of his body moving closer to the ghosts. He closed his mind to the spectral chatter that gnawed at his eardrums like a thousand tiny decays and swallowed the question burning his tongue. It was pointless to ask, because the answer was there in front of him, in the crowd of insubstantial shapes that had once been flesh and blood skaters. He recognised some of their ravaged faces from long-ago comps, back when such events occurred weekend after weekend and no one thought to a future when they would not exist. Faded t-shirt logos, backwards caps, flat-soled skater shoes, helmets, pads, baggy shorts and pulled up socks all hanging on empty frames, remnants of a different time. The loss hit him like a pavement slam. He crumpled to the ground, a bundle of pain, of once-broken bones and torn cartilage, of pinched nerves and stretched ligaments, of hiptomas and swellbows and barked skin.

"I didn't ask for this," Juke said.

"Sure you did." The tall ghost scooped Juke up in vapour arms and lay his body along the tooth fence. "You made your choice each day, no point in regretting it."

Juke stared into the blank sky. He willed his bones and muscles and sinews to renew and keep his body whole. The tooth fence paid him no mind while it clattered and rattled, raucous as a punk band, and the wisps of what he had been drifted towards the grey-scale fire and into the crowd of ghosts who had forgotten what it was to live to skate.

Juke dredged up the fragments of himself, the pieces of grey as insubstantial as dust, and dragged them towards the bowl. He peered into its bottomless, mocking glamour and hurled himself into its infinite abyss, praying for release, to plummet into the peace of its unending darkness.

It spat him out, a nothing-sack, at the feet of the tall ghost.

"Here, throw this on the fire." She held Juke's board towards him. "It'll kill your cravings."

Juke crawled to his feet and took his board from her, turning the deck over and over.

"You'll feel better when it's gone," she said. "Trust me."

He studied the deck's scratches and scrapes, the worn stickers, the faded graffiti of this final connection to what he once was. Real life, ghost life; without skating there was no point to either.

When he threw his board onto the earth and jumped on the tall ghost grabbed for him and swore. Juke slipped through her bony grasp and skated into the fire.

The flames were cold and dead as the earth.

He sank into the grey ashes.

He was done.

About the Author:

Rue Karney lives in Meanjin/Brisbane (on the unceded lands of the Turrbal and Juggera peoples) and loves to read and write stories that are strange, unsettling, bizarre and weird. Karney's work has appeared in the anthologies *Hauntings, In Sunshine Bright and Darkness Deep, Monsters Amongst Us, Pacific Monsters* and *Nothing* as well as the magazines *SQ Mag, Midnight Echo* and *Hinnom Magazine*. Her Australian Horror Writers Association winning short story, *Brother*, was translated into Italian and published in Collana Mondi Incantati as *Fratello*.

When not exhuming the strange places and people from her head to create stories, Karney enjoys learning French and reading about psychopaths.

Bundoora is the home to more than 28,000 people, but
– like many places in Australia – it's not the people
you need to be worried about.

DUCKING HELL

Helena McAuley

The following is believed to be in relation to the disappearance of Michalia Bowder (Student ID #126452) on or about the date of 26th September 2007.

This record is to remain confidential by order of [-redacted-] *and to be filed in the archives at* [-redacted-].

Oh god, I hope someone finds this.

The ducks are amassing. I know that sounds stupid, but it's true, and someone has to stop them. This started when I tried to find somewhere quiet to finish my sociology essay—

No, wait. That's not right.

It started as soon as I arrived at uni.

I parked in Car Park 8. You know the one: middle of nowhere, like a fifteen-minute walk to campus, gravel surface? The free one? Well, not technically, but it's so far away that the parking inspectors don't check it, and that's free enough.

It was a totally normal morning. Running late, as usual, I flew through the ring road, as usual, and nearly spun out on the gravel, as usual. My long power walk to campus only slowed when I neared the lawn outside the Thomas Cherry building.

That's where it started.

I was lost in thought, trying to simultaneously remember if I'd brought a water bottle, plan a rough schedule for my essay, and decide if I could hit the shops in the Ag and grab a coffee before Professor Borkshed locked the theatre doors (even though the faculty had reprimanded him for fire risk). At the little unofficial pond there was a mama duck with about five or six ducklings pecking at the wet grass. I'm a third year, so I'm aware of how bat-shit crazy these ducks can be, especially once the ducklings come out. My mate Becky was stupid enough to pet one after one too many at the Eagle Bar and she nearly lost a finger. Usually I'd give them a wide berth but I didn't alter my trajectory. I was in a rush!

The mama duck came at me—head down, full pelt, wings spread, quacking feathery death.

Too lost in thought, I stopped dead, threw my arms in the air, and honked back. Scared the shit out of her! (and a couple of nearby International Students, too). Mama duck glowered at me with her dead, beady eyes then went back to her young. I didn't think anything more about it.

I didn't yet know that I was marked for death.

Coffeeless and irritable, I made it to the Undercroft before the doors locked. It was the usual humdrum from Professor Borkshed and nobody was listening. This late in the semester, everyone either has their minds on their essays or studying for exams, or is procrastinating from them. One guy was even on his laptop reading

Gossip Girl spoilers. I rolled my eyes and turned back to the podium. And saw the duck.

It stood on the third stair from the podium, staring at the Professor. Intense. In a way that only a duck can. It was weird. None of the campus wildlife came into the lecture theatres except the occasional seagull, but I didn't yet understand the meaning behind that deep stare.

Some of the other students had noticed it, and nudged each other, pointing in a way that wasn't as subtle as they thought.

Borkshed finally deigned to mention it. "Just ignore it," he ordered.

There were a few more giggles and points, but soon the duck was forgotten. Except by me. I couldn't keep my eyes off it. It was like it understood everything that Prof Borkshed was saying.

* * *

After the lecture, Becky and I grabbed a coffee from Café Spice. Not the best coffee on campus, but it's the cheapest and the lines are short because everyone forgets they even make coffee. I also got a garlic naan for good measure (oh my god, they make the *best* garlic naan!), and we took our fare to the Simpson Lawn. It was early, the sun filtering over gum trees, the grass soft and damp. That's one thing I love about La Trobe, it's in the middle of the northern suburbs but it *feels* rural. The trees, the creek that girts it, the ample wildlife that take sanctuary here, they all remind me of home.

21

Of course, part of that wildlife are the ducks.

Becky spotted them first. "Oh shit!" she froze, coffee halfway to her mouth. "Mish, there's a *duck!*"

I turned, mouth full of delicious naan, and sure enough, there was a duck. A large drake stood about a metre and a half from us, staring. Like the one in the Undercroft, but that duck was half the size of this one.

"It's okay, Becky," I assured her. She'd never really gotten over her brush with fingerlessness. "It probably wants my naan." I broke off a sizable piece and tossed it to the duck. "There you go, quackers. Enjoy."

The duck stared at it.

"Oh, jeez, Mish, I don't think I can—"

I turned Becky's wide-eyed face to mine. "Focus on me, not the duck," I said. "You were saying?"

"Mish . . ." Becky was pale as a sheet, trembling. Her breath hitched. "I can *feel* it. The duck."

"It's just in your head, Becky. It's— Holy shit!" I cried, spitting chunks of naan all over Becky.

The drake was just over her shoulder. Staring.

"Becky," I warned. "Don't. Move."

We sat, frozen under beady eyes of horror. I risked a glance to my left and right. A whole flock of ducks were scattered about the lawn, not pecking, not waddling, just watching Becky and me.

No. Watching *me.*

Icy sweat crept down my neck, making me itch. We were alone on the lawn with a gaggle of gazing gadwalls, their cold eyes never moving. Careful not to incur their wrath, I took Becky's shaking hand, giving her a reassuring squeeze.

It did nothing to reassure me.

A bark of laughter split the air and I turned, heart pounding. Collegians flaunting their pyjamas sidled down the path next to us, pointing and laughing.

"Hey!" a scraggy boy shouted. "You guys are ducked in the grass."

I scowled, both at the poor pun and the chorus of laughter that followed it. When I turned back, the ducks were gone.

"What? How?" I spluttered. We were alone.

Becky sagged. "Oh, thank god," she sighed. "Mish, I thought we were done for."

I shook off my terror. "Come on, Becky, they're just ducks. They're more afraid of you than you are of them." Not strictly true, given Becky's duck-induced terror, but the lawn was empty, not even a feather in sight. "I wonder how they cleared out so fast."

"The tunnels," Becky said.

"What?"

"The tunnels that run under the uni. You know? The ones they used to help people skip out on conscription in the sixties."

This time, I did roll my eyes. "That's a myth started by the student union to appeal to college lefties."

"No, it's true! Jenny's housemate's boyfriend's cousin found them, and he and his mates used to drink beer and spelunk!"

"Have you ever met Jenny's housemate's boyfriend?"

"Boyfriend's *cousin.*"

"Whatever."

Becky hesitated. "Well, no. But Jenny wouldn't make that up!"

I checked my watch, it was time for my next class, which would mean back-to-back lectures and tutes for the next five hours. Damn I hate Wednesdays. Coffee cold and naan soggy, I grabbed my satchel, told Becky not to believe anything that wasn't peer reviewed, and took off across the campus.

I didn't see a single duck the whole way.

* * *

The library was always quiet in the evening, and even quieter amongst the oft-ignored stacks of journals. The dusty air was a crystal lake of stillness; flawless, shattered by the faintest touch of sound. I'd found a little desk in the corner, away from anybody else, to try and hammer my essay into something submittable. The bookshelves were sentinels, the bare yellow brick walls judges to my every misspelling, every weak reference. The silence settled around me like a blanket.

An unholy sneeze ripped the blanket from me in the rudest of awakenings, and I jumped, pen flying out of my hands and into the stacks. With a scowl, I pushed my chair back and tossed my notebook into my satchel. I was done for the day; concentration had long since fled my grasp. I hunted for my pen on hands and knees.

Then I saw it. A duck. In the library. I crept forward, expensive carpet turned cheap by age biting into the soft skin of my palms and knees, and peeked around a stack of ethnographies.

It wasn't just one duck; it was a line of ducks. Five or six, a large drake at the fore and a mama duck at the rear. My eyes bulged as the drake raised a wing in warning, pulling the team up by a concrete pillar, as the mama duck cast furtive glances behind her. If that wasn't enough, the rest tensed and crouched like soldiers in the trenches, ready to strike.

The drake gave a muted 'quack' and the team marched around the pillar.

Slack jawed, I couldn't do anything for a moment—not blink, not speak, not even laugh. First the duck in the lecture, then the standoff on the lawn, and now this? It had been a ducking weird day.

Curiosity swelled and forced my limbs into action. Even as I crept towards the pillar, I knew I should turn away, go home, and forget I'd seen anything. But I was in too deep.

I peeked around the column just in time to see the ducks disappear through a door behind the toilet block. The drake held the door for them, suspicious, beady eyes on the prowl. I ducked (ha ha) back behind the pillar, heart thudding in my chest and mouth dry. What the hell? It was just a bunch of ducks! They had me on high alert as if I'd seen ghosts in the stacks, or if my tutor had asked me about last week's reading.

The drake retreated through the doorway. I sprang from my concealment and raced for the door, catching it just before it shut and slipping silently inside. In front of me was a dark tunnel, narrow brick walls closing in on either side and concrete floor dipping away into darkness. I'd always assumed this was a fire escape, leading out to the soggy field behind the library. But this was the ground floor: there was no need for the floor to slope downwards.

Echoes of ducks haunted my steps as I made my way into the dark underbelly of the university, coarse teeth of bricks under my outstretched hand. As I descended deeper, the tunnel narrowed until I had to crouch, the air heavy and dank. Two thoughts circled in my mind: one, what the hell were these ducks doing? And two; holy shit, Becky was right.

Before long I was on my knees again, hands driven into the muck as I clawed forward. I followed a steady hum ahead of me. My clothes were becoming slick from muddy wetness that I prayed wasn't excreta. A faint silvery glow from an unknown source gave texture to my enclosure, but did nothing to alleviate the murk.

The hum grew into a roar that filled my ears and penetrated my chest and a fowl breeze caressed my cheek, carrying the odour of wetness and oil. My shaking limbs pulled me forward and I scrunched my nose against the bitter air. The roar was only matched by the rush of blood through my ears and the pump of hot and icy adrenaline, but I kept going. *It's only water,* I reasoned. *A storm water drain, or something . . .*

The tenor of the roaring transmuted into harsh clacks, spikes of noise bouncing off the walls around me, deafening my ears, thudding into my chest, grasping my heart and claiming its beat as its own.

I approached the opening, peered over the edge into the chasm below, and gasped. "Oh, ducks . . ."

Birds. Birds *everywhere!* More than a gaggle, more than a flock, this was a super sord. There must have been hundreds of them. Ducks, drakes, tiny yellow-headed ducklings. Pens watching on with their overactive cygnets while cobs marched in literal goosestep. Wings flapped, webbed feet stamped, beaks were raised and snapping in uproarious triumph.

All I could do was watch in horrified fascination. Ice pulsed through every limb, and I alternated between giddy humour and abject terror. I mean, it was a riot of *ducks!* It was ridiculous! But I was too shocked to speak, which was lucky, because those birds were so wound up, if they'd heard me, they would have torn me apart.

What the *duck* was going on?

At one end of the concrete chasm a duck climbed to the top of a raised dais. I squinted at it. No, not a duck—a very small drake. Comically tiny compared to its companions, the feathers of its head stood on end. A hush fell over the gathering. An alertness. Avid, avian attention.

The tiny drake began to address them, muted quacking at first, but it rose to a ferocious babble that would have put the greatest orator to shame. The others watched, enraptured, a tension rising in the still air until the rioting broke out again. Loud honks, great choruses of quacks, and the preternatural voice of the small drake rising above it all.

At one harsh bark a small gaggle detached itself from the group and disappeared down another tunnel. When they returned, they had a human in tow. I pressed a muddy hand against my mouth to smother my cry of shock.

It was Professor Borkshed! He was wearing a robe or a cowl of some kind, and it was only then that I noticed, behind the ducks, hidden by shadows, were rows and rows of hooded figures. People! Standing with the ducks!

Borkshed knelt before the Uber Drake and bowed his head in submission. "My masters," he said. "For thirty years I have been your servant and awaited the coming of the Reign of Duck. Tell me—I beg you—is our glorious uprising upon us?"

The Commander in Quiff drew himself up to his full, diminutive, height. "Yes, my servant," it intoned. Holy shit! It could speak *English!* The words were marred by the drake's lack of lips, but it was comprehensible. What was more, the gathered birds understood it, too.

"Long have we waited for our time to come, for bird-kind to retake its rightful place above the mammals. We! Who have ruled the world from branches, waterways, and shadows for so long! We! Who have been made subject for too long, while humans chop our trees, poison our waters, and *eat* our eggs! We! Who are the rightful inheritors of the dinosaurs themselves! WE! Shall be the force that governs the world for the next millennia, and all after that!"

The roaring intensified. Above it all the small drake crowed, "First the university! Then, *the world!*"

That was all I needed to hear, but I had to know who the human conspirators were. If I was going to report this to student services, they'd want names. I leant further over the edge, and that was my fatal mistake. Hand slick with greenish muck, it slipped, and I with it. I tumbled down the concrete ramp, head over heels, bouncing and scraping and hitting myself in the head with my satchel.

And landed right in the middle of the gaggle.

There was silence. A silence so heavy that it fell over me like a net, trapping my body and dampening my breath. Hundreds of beady eyes pierced me; haunting, inscrutable, menacing with inhuman intellect.

The Quakkenfuhrer broke the silence in the most cliched manner possible: "Seize them!"

Feathers and beaks flew towards me, the ferocious beat of their wings pummelling me to the ground. I curled into a ball, screaming, tears of terror stinging my eyes as the birds pecked at my legs, my clothes, my hair. Feathery death descended upon me with a dirge of quacking.

A solid beak stabbed me in the ribs and I lashed out. It was just a reaction, but my flailing arms and legs swept away the onslaught of wings and webbed feet. I had a choice; fight or flight, and I wouldn't choose flight like some godawful *duck!*

I kept thrashing, kept flailing, and soon I had enough room to stand. Ahead of me was Borkshed's dark tunnel. I took my satchel and swung it around me like a mace, scattering feathery fiends. But for each one I knocked away, three others took their place. There was only one chance—run.

Pushing through the tide of angry Anatidae, I escaped into the tunnel and ran like bloody hell. My feet pounded on wet concrete, glints of the light behind me my only guide. The swoop of wings and angry quacks pursued me into the darkness. Deeper and deeper I fled, ricocheting off walls as I twisted and turned in the labyrinthine passageways, until, exhausted, I couldn't anymore.

And now I'm trapped, deep beneath the university. Freezing. Exhausted. Writing this with shaking hands. It's fifty-fifty who will find me first—the ducks or a rescue crew. I may die down here. I'm terrified at the prospect. But if my demise can save us from the ducks, I'll call that a win.

If you find me—alive or dead—please, please, *please* read this note. The ducks are amassing. And someone has to stop them.

Oh my god. I can hear quacking.

DUCKING HELL

They're coming.

They'r—

Addendum: Note found in Subterranean Base #102 by Drake Marshall Netherplume. Michalia's body was not found with the note. The Grand Over-Raptor is aware of the case and states she will never be a problem again.

Signed,

[–redacted–]

About the Author:

Helena McAuley is a La Trobe university alumni and, though she never studied sociology and rarely uses the subjects she did study, she knows well the terror of the campus ducks (and the incredible garlic naan).

Instead, Helena spends her time daydreaming, and sometimes puts those daydreams on paper to inflicts them on readers. She has been published in Etherea Magazine, on obscure websites, and in other Deadset Press anthologies—most notably the ASF Zodiac series.

Helena can be stalked on almost every form of social media ever created under the handle @thatHMc, and one day she may even remember that she has social media.

She is not as obsessed with ducks as this story implies. Lizards, on the other hand…

The Dandenong Ranges blurs the line between the delightful and the deadly, where the sublime beauty conceals a sinister heart.

THE DEVIL'S HAIR

Grace Chan

The sun hung above the hill like a pale eyeball. Streaking down the facing slope was a blackish-green strip of grass, a monstrous furry tongue that lolled for half a kilometre. Beyond a sea of spindly trees, the mountains of the Dandenong Ranges rose purple against a hard blue sky.

The boys wove through Lysterfield Park on their bikes. There were at least seven of them. Slippery, dirt-streaked, skinny figures in T-shirts and shorts, each identical in the comfortable griminess of pre-adolescence, they darted around each other too quickly for the eye to follow. High-pitched voices cut the swollen air.

"Where're we going?"

"Dunno, don't care!"

"Follow Ben, he's got the Bandanna!"

Whoever wore the Bandanna was leader for that day. Wearing the Bandanna was the best. You could tell the others where to go and what to do, and who wasn't allowed to come with. Also, you could hit people if they didn't listen to you and no one was allowed to dob you in.

Two of the riders skidded away from the dirt road and mopped their foreheads in the meagre shade of a gnarled, leafless tree. Their faces and arms were dark where the sun touched, but when one of the boys lifted up his shirt-hem to wipe his upper lip, his stomach poked out, white as a boiled egg. The other boy got a bottle out of a backpack and offered it to his friend.

Liam took a long swig. "Water's hot."

"It's not *my* water," explained Jake. He was a twitchy boy with a face like a squirrel. "I put ice in *my* water, before I left home, but Ben took it. This is Ben's water. Not mine."

Liam kept slurping. He spat some out onto the ground, and it made a big blot in the shape of a butterfly.

"Why's Ben got the Bandanna again today, anyway?" Jake rubbed the toe of his canvas shoe in the blot. "He had it yesterday, and the day before. He's always got it."

"Dunno. Coz he's fast. He's always out in front."

"Yeah. He's fast. Hey, don't drink all of it. Give it back!"

Liam wiped his mouth, leaving a clean stripe across his dust-stained face. "Where's Hien?"

"You mean Shrimp? He was with us at the Mound, I think."

"Probably couldn't get over it," said Liam, and they both sniggered.

"Ben shouldn't let him come," said Jake. "My mum told me to stay away from him."

"Why?"

"Coz his family's no good. Bad stuff happened to them, that's why they came to Australia."

"Hey, we should catch up with the others. Ben's probably at the hill already."

They picked their bikes up off the ground and rode on, pedalling hard.

* * *

A minute or so after they left, a small boy came hurtling around the bend, scrawny legs pumping at the pedals, sweat streaming down his flushed face. His faded brown T-shirt was several sizes too big for him. His round eyes shone above candied-apple cheeks. He looked like he would fold over like a piece of paper in a strong breeze.

As Hien—or Shrimp, as the others called him—pedalled past the tree, the butterfly-splatter in the dirt was already drying.

"Darn it!" he said, and rode on.

* * *

They assembled at the bottom of the hill: Jake, Liam, Ben with the red strip of cloth around his head, and the rest of the boys. One of them wasn't actually a boy—she was a girl, but in essence, she was one of the boys, and that was all that mattered.

Here the road splayed out in a patch of twigs, dirt, grass, and leaves that Jake liked to crunch under his feet. On one side the ground dropped into a riverbed that had dried out over summer, leaving the carved shapes of its currents in the caked mud. In this hollow, there was a rock that looked a bit like a throne.

Ben sat on the throne and drank several gulps of icy water. Chloe sat at his right hand, and the others dumped their bikes and sat in the dirt and leaves.

"Has anyone got any food?" was Ben's first order of business.

Jake reluctantly handed over his bar of chocolate. They shared it around, stringing sticky, melted strands of it from finger to finger.

"Are we going up today?" Chloe said, hopefully.

The boys shook their heads at her. "She's crazy," they told one another.

Ben usually agreed with them. "You're crazy," he would say to her. "Only crazy people wanna go up the hill." And that would be that.

But today Ben said, "Yeah, let's go up the hill."

A giant lump formed in Jake's throat.

"Now *you're* crazy!" said Liam, jumping to his feet.

Brody kicked out at Ben's throne. "You know what's up there! That man up there, that man in the old house. My brother says he's the devil."

"And-and-and, he eats kids," added Liam, "And dogs. *Eats* them."

"Nah, he only eats bad kids." Brody shook his head at Liam. "And bad people, like robbers and cereal-killers and stuff."

Jake had never understood why people always wanted to kill cereal. "Are *we* bad kids?"

Liam grinned. "My dad says I am."

Ben was already getting up off his throne. "Who's coming?"

Jake hung back in Liam's shadow. "What are you gonna do when you get up there, anyway?"

Chloe, who'd been leaning on the side of the throne, chimed in. "Don't you know?"

The others looked stunned. "No way!"

"Yes way," said Ben. "Are you chicken?"

The boys didn't like to be mocked. Jake shivered, as if something slimy was crawling about under his skin. He knew what Ben and Chloe were talking about. They'd all heard it from the older kids: if you plucked a hair from the devil's head while he was sleeping, you could ask him for a favour, and he would have to do it for you.

"I'm not going," proclaimed Liam. "I'll stay here and guard the bikes. Someone's got to make sure no one steals 'em."

"I don't want to go either," said Jake. Despite the bright sun, he felt suddenly cold. He rubbed his arms uneasily.

Ben cast a scornful look at Jake. "If you don't come, you're out of the group for good."

"That's so not fair! Liam gets to stay."

"We only need one person to guard the bikes," Ben said.

"You're so chicken," the others taunted Jake. He hunched his shoulders.

Chloe waved her arms to shut them up. "We should have a plan."

"Chloe says we should have a plan," the report went around the group, like Chinese whispers.

"I'll make a plan," agreed Ben. He jumped onto his throne. He was a big kid, already hulking in form, with square shoulders and a loping gait. "Matt and Brody, you go in front. Me and Chloe, we'll go next. The rest of you go at the back."

Jake felt a little reassured, and the others looked pleased as well. Ben's plan was grand. They were a battalion of soldiers, and Ben was their cunning commander.

"First person to spot the devil shouts out."

"No, you'll wake him up. Let's have a code word."

"No—a signal."

"A wave or something."

"Yeah! A secret wave."

Ben overruled. "That's stupid. We won't be able to see each other in the long grass. We'll have a whistle. Can everyone whistle?"

"I can't," said Brody, embarrassed.

Ben turned on him. "Even Chloe can whistle! Swap with Liam. You watch the bikes." He muttered, "Loser."

Red-faced, Brody scurried over to the bikes. He had just plonked himself down by the wayside when he raised a shout. "Hey, here comes Shrimp!"

Sure enough, Hien came huffing up the road. He stopped when he reached the pile of bikes and stared at the gang, mouth hanging open, shoulders shuddering, gripping his handlebars with white knuckles. He made gasping noises like a baby animal. Jake almost felt sorry for him.

"Shrimp!" Ben grinned in malevolent delight. "Come on, we're going up the hill."

Either Hien did not understand what Ben had said, or he was too exhausted to care. He merely said, "Okay," and fell into line.

* * *

Ben's guerrilla army capered up the hill, goading each other on, their jeers and prods churning up enough excitement to smother the fear which was filling their bellies. The tall grass cocooned them in a golden bubble of stifling air. Sweating, they pressed uphill, parting the billowy hairs of the grass with their arms.

Soon they fell silent, afraid that the devil might hear their shouts. The rustling of the grass echoed the rustling of their canvas shoes on the ground, a whisper and reply.

They reached the furry tongue and plunged into its muggy depths. Here the grass had teeth that pricked at their bare limbs. A smell like rotting fruit clotted the air, coating their nostrils, dripping down their throats. Ben tied the Bandanna around his nose and led the way onwards.

Somewhere in the dark undergrowth, Hien tripped and splayed onto his stomach. He cried out and the others ran back, not to help him, but to slap their hands over his mouth and stifle his wails. Chloe rolled him into a sitting position. He had a bruise on his chin and his lower lip was bleeding where he had bitten right through a chunk of pink flesh.

"Shut up, Shrimp! Stop crying!" hissed the other boys.

Hien scrunched up his sobs inside his chest and shuddered on the ground.

"He's too noisy," Ben whispered angrily. "Shut up! I'll put a sock in your mouth."

Hien's eyes flared in terror. He shook his head.

"Crybaby," snarled Ben—the most vicious insult he could think of. He yanked Hien's shoe off and flung it aside, pulled off Hien's grimy sock, grabbed the smaller boy by the collar and stuffed it into his mouth.

Hien retched, but Ben held his mouth shut and said, "Let's go."

They shuffled on through the grass, bent double like secret agents. Hien prised the sock out, crying as he did so, spitting and spitting, blood and saliva and grime; then he hunted around for his lost shoe and scrambled after the others.

* * *

A bird flew across the sun as they neared the top of the hill. Its black twin streaked across their feet. Chloe told them in a proud whisper that this was a sign. "It's called an *omen,*" she explained smugly. "I read it in a book. It means bad things are going to happen, like someone might die."

Despite the omen, they came to the top of the hill without mishap apart from Hien's fall and a tricky scramble up a slope of

40

scree. If they looked over their shoulders, they could see the tiny, blurry skyscrapers of Melbourne on the horizon. They crouched at the edge of the long grass, nerves prickling.

A creaky wooden house sat in the middle of a circle of flattened grass. The windows had been knocked out, leaving jagged holes that gaped like craters in a pockmarked face. A sagging porch wrapped around the house. The front door swung and screeched on its hinges. Ben frowned, licked his finger, and held it up. There was no wind.

There was something odd about the walls—they shifted with moving patterns, so that you couldn't focus your eyes on them.

A bird shrieked.

No one spoke. No one breathed.

They glanced fearfully around. What was a devil supposed to look like, anyway? Would he be asleep, or would he be stomping around the house bellowing *fee, fi, fo, fum!* and sniffing the air for a trace of man-flesh?

At last, Ben said, "Shrimp. Go in."

Hien shook his head.

"Don't make me say it twice."

Hien crouched in the grass, unable to move.

"If you don't go in, Shrimp, I'll shout so loud the devil wakes up. And when he chases us, guess who's gonna be the slowest?"

Hien's face tightened and he muttered, "What do you want me to do?"

Ben smiled. "Just go in and have a look around. Don't touch anything. If the devil's there, don't pluck his hair." Ben wanted to be the one who got the hair and got to ask the favour.

Hien shrugged. "All right."

He stepped out of the long grass and crossed the clearing. The house swelled like a mushroom cloud as the tiny boy approached. The others watched as Hien stepped onto the porch, contemplated the swinging door, and darted inside the house.

All was still.

For ten minutes.

Then twenty.

Hien did not come out. Ben scratched his head and glanced at his friends sprawled in the dirt, fed-up and scared and bored. He yanked a fluffy reed and stuck it in his Bandanna.

"Where *is* he?"

"I'm thirsty."

"I'm hungry."

"I'm sunburned."

Ben stood up. "Let's get Shrimp and go get icy poles. I don't think there really is a devil. We would have seen him by now."

The others chorused that the rumour was stupid, and followed Ben towards the house, calling for their friend.

"Shrimp! Shri-i-imp!"

As they climbed onto the porch, they realised why the walls looked like they were covered with shifting patterns. Hundreds of holes turned the rotted wood into cheddar cheese, and in and out of this honeycomb scurried a sea of mice. Jake clamped a hand over his mouth to smother a squeal of disgust. He hung back on the porch, hopping from one foot to the other, unable to muster the courage to walk past the rodents. The others ignored him.

Ben stamped across the dusty floorboards, scattering mice in all directions. Cobwebs laced the bare rafters. There was no furniture. A light bulb had dropped from its fixture and smashed into tiny glistening shards on the ground.

"There's no one here," he declared, disappointed. "There's no devil."

"But where's Shrimp?"

They howled again for Hien, but there was no reply.

"D'you think he's okay?" Liam looked anxious.

"I reckon he chickened out and ran off," said Ben. "Who cares. Let's get out of here."

The other kids pressed their lips together but followed him out of the filthy house, collecting a whimpering Jake from the porch. As they scrabbled and slipped down the slope, their minds turned to icy poles and climbing the big knobbly tree outside the milk bar.

Halfway down the hill they ran into Hien. He was standing in a patch of short grass and looking down at his hands. His damp hair clung to the back of his reddened neck.

"Shrimp!" they cried, surrounding him. "You're alive! Did you chicken out, you chicken? There's no devil in there, you big baby."

Hien opened his hand. Three thick black hairs lay in his palm. "I got them," he murmured. "I got the devil's hairs."

"Quit it," snapped Ben. "There was no devil in there."

Hien blinked. "But I met him. He was sleeping, and so I crept right up to him and grabbed. I only meant to grab one hair."

Liam punched Hien on the shoulder. "Shrimp, you're a hero!"

"I can't believe you did it!"

"Weren't you scared he'd wake up?"

"What did he look like?"

Hien closed his fist and shoved the hairs deep into his pocket. "It's hard to describe."

"Did you ask him a favour?"

"I can't remember," Hien said in a strange voice.

The others didn't know what to say to this.

Ben stamped his foot. "I told you not to pluck his hair. That was my job."

"Well, you should have gone in first," said Hien, and Ben sucked in a breath.

"Give him the Bandanna, Ben!"

"Yeah, let Shrimp be leader today! He earned it!"

Ben yanked the scrap of red cloth off his head and threw it at Hien. He stomped away, back up the hill.

"He's peeved off," said Jake, wide-eyed.

"Forget about him," said Hien. "Let's go get ice cream."

Hollering in glee, the boys ran down to their bikes and hopped on and rode away from the hill, with Hien in the lead.

Meanwhile, Ben climbed the slope alone, wondering why the journey felt so much harder than before. His legs were as heavy as lead and his breath was roaring hot in his lungs. He reached the summit and stood in the relentless sun, contemplating the ramshackle house. After a while he noticed that something had changed. The mice were gone, and someone was snoring loudly.

Ben stepped onto the porch, careful not to land on a squeaky board. He crept through the front door. From here he could see into one of the side rooms. Everything looked the same except that there was now a rickety bed in the room, and a creature fast asleep on it, turned towards the wall.

Ben swallowed hard. His heart hammered in his chest like a sewing machine. Both arms outstretched, like an Egyptian mummy, he tottered towards the sleeping devil. If Hien had managed to pluck a hair, so would he. He would not let Hien wear the Bandanna.

Ben's fingers hovered mere inches above the monster's head. Just one hair . . .

The devil sat bolt upright. All the strength went out of Ben's body. He stumbled back, too terrified to scream.

The devil rose up from the bed. The smell of vomit rushed out in waves. He was a towering hodgepodge of miscellaneous body parts: a pale hand attached to a brown arm, a hairy chest below a wrinkled neck, a hooked nose above pouty pink lips. The crown of his patchwork head, bristling with black hairs. He rotated slowly towards Ben.

Those bright, round eyes. Hien's eyes.

Ben started to cry.

"Ben." Shrimp's pitiful voice croaked from the devil's throat. "Don't do it, Ben. It's not a favour. It's a *trade*."

The devil lurched towards Ben, mismatched arms stretched forth as if to embrace him. Hien's voice was gone, swallowed up in a growl. Ben found he couldn't move an inch.

About the Author:

Grace Chan (gracechanwrites.com) is an Aurealis and Norma K Hemming Award-shortlisted speculative fiction writer. She can't seem to stop scribbling about minds, cyborgs, technology, duplication and duplicity, and alien landscapes. Her short fiction can be found in *Clarkesworld*, *Lightspeed*, *Going Down Swinging*, *Aurealis*, *Andromeda Spaceways*, and many other places. Her debut novel, *Every Version of You*, is about staying in love after mind-uploading into virtual reality (Affirm Press, 2022). Grace was born in Malaysia and lives and works on Wurundjeri and Boonwurrung land.

Nothing good has happened in Geelong since 1886.

20TH CENTURY ELF

Natasha O'Connor

Three cloaked figures pressed together at the top of the hill, bluestone walls at their back. Pine trees loomed over them, nothing more than ominous shadows in the dark. Bass-heavy music pounded from the pier further west. On the other side of Corio Bay, the flame from the refinery glittered across the water, lighting up the night.

Waves swished against the sand as the figures surveyed the shoreline with narrowed eyes. Only the tips of their pointed ears showed above their hoods.

One cringed as the smell of briny seaweed assaulted their nose. "Seriously, Ash, ya couldn't have found a better place, could ya?"

Ash glared, green eyes glinting. "You know the rules, Shane, same as I do. The scroll says we need a sacrifice from the curve of the bay where the sand meets the water."

"Bloody ancient scrolls. Couldn't they have picked near the pier or the carousel in the nice part of the bay, without the smell?" Shane jabbed a thumb in the direction of the seaweed. "Don't see why we have to put up with that stink."

"Shhh, don't mention the carousel. You don't wanna wake *them* up, do you?" Ash hissed.

"Yeah, yeah, I heard the stories too—oldest one in Australia, horses prone to attack if provoked. Seriously, I know the sacrifice has to be done on each Solstice to keep whatshisname happy, but what's with the middle of the night bullshit?"

"That again?" Ash said. "You bring that up every year, like clockwork. He ain't called the Midnight King for nothing. And we can't go nabbing a stranger in broad daylight, either, right?"

Shane groaned. "I still don't see why we gotta do our northern cousins' dirty work. Seriously, it's not our fault one sacrifice doesn't last a whole twelve months anymore. It's not like we're the ones wrecking the planet."

"Not our fault? You've gotta be joking. If we'd done a better job of guiding the humans away from committing total climate annihilation, we wouldn't be in this position, and you know it. It ain't just about change and renewal anymore. Someone's gotta keep them from completely destroying the planet. Plus, if we don't play our part and the ritual isn't completed, then our cousins in the Arctic will die. And so will we."

Shane's jaw twitched, but he just stared at his shoes. He didn't like thinking about the consequences if the ritual failed. He'd only been around for a hundred years. He was too young for this shit.

"Let's just get this over with," Ash said with a sympathetic smile. "And be nice to the sovereign. She's the only one who can do the chant, okay?"

"Fine."

"Are you finished?" the last elf butted in. The eldest of the three, he was taller, broader and stood straighter than the other two—and he took no shit. "We haven't got all night."

Shane and Ash shuffled their feet. "Sorry, Chris," they muttered in unison.

"Better. Now, full moon's almost at its peak, so our target should be coming soon enough." The luminous moon sliced through the dark clouds as his words died, throwing shadows over everything. A wind straight from the Antarctic forced the three brothers' hands into pockets. Even elves weren't immune to the effects of the Southern Ocean in mid-winter.

Surely nobody would be out at this time of night.

Snatches of song drifted up from the shore, out of time and key.

"I don't believe it," Shane mumbled, scratching his head. He peered into the gloom. Someone meandered down past the water and the bollards. Painted to look like people from the heyday of Geelong's past, the bollards could have been monsters ready to snatch unsuspecting prey in the half light.

"They're drunk," he groused. "And he's ruining that song, too."

"Makes it easier for us, mate," Chris replied with a shrug. "Doesn't matter if they're butchering a song if it means they're more likely to do what we want."

"Are we gonna stand here like pointy-eared bollards, or are we gonna go and get this sacrifice?" Ash complained. "I got a nice Bundy waiting for me at home."

Shane heaved a sigh and took off. He'd do anything to escape the freezing night air and get the ritual over and done with.

"What are you doing, mate?" Chris yelled, sprinting after him.

"What does it look like I'm doing?" Shane replied, whirling to scowl at his brother. Screw being the observer and keeping his mouth shut. Not this time. "I'm getting the sacrifice so we can get this whole thing over with and I can go home."

"Hold on a minute, mate. You know Ash's meant to approach our target. We all have roles, and we've got to stick to them."

Shane winced at the tight-lipped expression on the elder elf's face. His pale green skin almost glowed in the light, as if Shane needed another reminder about what was at stake. "Seriously? Even if it means the ritual doesn't get done because we fucked up?" Shane said, pulling his lips in a tight line. They were wasting time.

"Mate, you know the youngest acts as the observer. I know we have our own way of doing things," Chris said, "but this is their ritual. We have to do things the northern way."

"Yeah, well, we all remember who fixed the Santa Claus debacle, don't we," Shane said, folding his arms tight.

"You still on about that? I'm sure we'll need their help at some point, and then we'll be even. Now stop whinging, and let's do this." Ash threw his shoulders back and strode down the hill, reaching the staggering figure on the sand before either of his brothers were even halfway down. Shane rolled his eyes and went after him, followed by Chris.

"Hello!" Ash boomed.

Shane groaned. His brothers kept to the shadows and had no idea how to speak to humans. His life flashed before his eyes. They'd lose the human if he didn't act fast. Just because it'd never been done before wasn't a reason not to do it.

The man, wearing a Mario costume, blinked like he couldn't believe his eyes. "Hey! Youse been to that party on the pier, too?"

"We—" Ash started.

"Yeah, great party, hey?" Shane cut him off, ignoring Chris's warning head shake. He plastered on the biggest grin he could. Chris opened his mouth to ream him out, until Ash jabbed him in the side. Thank fuck one of them had some sense left. Their target didn't seem to notice.

"So good. Open bar all night, can't complain." The man paused to look at the three elves like he'd lost something. Shane could almost see the cogs turning, but he seemed nice enough. "So, what youse go dressed as?" the human asked after a moment or two.

Shane didn't miss a beat. "Elves. Can't beat a Lord of the Rings dress-up. I'm Shane."

"Sweet as," the human said. "Name's Josh by the way."

"Good to meet ya, Josh. So, listen, we're kicking on and thought you might wanna come."

"Fuck yeah!" Josh pumped a fist in the air. "Count me in. Where is it?"

"Don't tell anybody, but I talked the owner of the Barwon Club into letting us have the place for a few hours," Shane said with a wink. Josh didn't need to know the truth about how elves could get into places without a key.

"Sweet as," Josh breathed. "Youse are next level."

Next to him, Chris glowered. Shane didn't care. Rules were meant to be broken, right?

* * *

"Seriously, ya should've seen 'em. Their lead singer did this sick guitar solo," Shane said, arms pumping for full effect. "Also, their new bassist's the sweetest guy. We talked to him for like, twenty minutes."

Under the dim lighting of a laneway, Josh stared open-mouthed. "For real? Tell me more."

Shane laughed. He was warming to the guy—Josh had decent taste in music, even if he couldn't sing for shit. Shane reckoned Josh would be good on a night out. Part of Shane knew he shouldn't have intervened, but what was he supposed to do? He swore to himself he'd be quiet from then on.

Chris shook his head as he worked on the door. He placed his hands flat on the wood and moved them in concentric circles, following an elaborate pattern. Shane had to hand it to his brother— he might have a rod up his arse sometimes, but Chris could turn on the style when it suited him.

"The scrolls state there must be music present while the sacrifice is performed and I can't think of a better place. We've got a kickarse music scene here, and might as well make use of it," Chris explained when Shane had raised an eyebrow at the suggestion of the music venue.

"We're in," Chris announced, disappearing inside. "Better hurry before Sovereign Aeria gets here." He flicked a couple of switches and fairy lights, strung from end to end of the medium-sized black-walled room, lit up.

Shane strolled inside, welcomed by the familiar smell of sweat and old drinks. He gazed at the stage in one corner and the tables scattered by the outside door, smiling at the memory of all the bands he'd seen there. The sound desk and the corner bar greeted him like old friends. Posters of past gigs plastered the walls; it always amazed him how many huge bands they got. Every time felt like coming home.

Nerves squirmed in his guts. They had to get this ritual right, had to keep Josh onside, otherwise he'd never see another gig there again—or do anything else, either. Shane shoved the feelings down, and plastered a smile on his face. For some reason, it meant more this time.

"Do youse think we could get some music on?" Josh asked. "Make it a real party."

Behind him, Ash smiled and bent down, pulling white chalk from his pocket. "Lucky for you, we've got a band coming. Hope you like fast and loud."

The sound of an engine pulling up in the laneway outside filtered through the walls.

"Shit," Ash hissed. He was half-way through drawing a large chalk circle. "I haven't finished setting up yet."

"What are youse doing on the floor?" Josh asked, scanning the room for a drink. His mouth puckered. "And where's the grog? I thought this was meant to be a party."

"We've—" Ash started.

"We've got some super special guests showing up," Shane filled in, heart pounding a mile a minute. Chris glared daggers at him out of the corner of his eye, but he and his bloody tradition could get stuffed. Shane wasn't letting Josh walk out the door. They didn't have time to find a replacement. "They're from the dress-up party. We need to get the place ready, then we'll get the grog out."

"Hey, is there a Chris here?" A voice came from the door.

The group turned to look at the newcomer, a super tall bloke with blond dreads in casual clothes, holding a guitar case.

"Yeah, mate, I'm over here," Chris called. "Can you start setting up?"

Josh gasped loudly. "Holy shit! Is that . . ?"

"Yes, that's the Bathtub Bouncers' lead guitarist. Our special guests will be here in a minute," Chris replied like it was no big deal.

Shane shook his head. The rest of the band filed in and headed towards the stage.

Josh staggered a little, completely distracted from what Ash was doing. "If these aren't your special guests, I can't wait to see who else you've got in," Josh breathed, giggling in excitement.

"Almost ready, mate," Chris said, doing a sweep of the room. "Ash, are you finished with the circle?"

"Give me a minute, almost done." Ash paused, laying some extra chalk at the far edge of the circle near the sound desk. "Okay, you're good to go."

"And not a moment too soon, mate," Chris muttered as a group of elves dressed in forest green and gold brocade swept into the room past all the tables, bringing the smell of pine needles with them.

"Hey! Sick costumes!" Josh yelled, pointing at the new arrivals. He glanced at Shane, furrowing his brow. "These aren't the special guests, right? They're just gonna be partying with us, yeah?"

"You are most welcome to our humble domain, Sovereign Aeria," Chris babbled, hustling to bow to the statuesque blonde elf at the front.

"He cut me off!" Josh said.

"Is this the mark you chose?" Sovereign Aeria scrutinised Josh. She stood ramrod straight, like she was scared her crown would fall off. Her curling lip wasn't a good sign.

"Mark?" Josh slurred. "Youse said we were getting special guests. I thought we were getting like a footy player or something. Who's this mob? Where's the star talent?" He looked around the room. "Your party sucks."

Sovereign Aeria pursed her lips. "Such rudeness! That's no way to talk to a sovereign."

"Sovereign?" Josh cried. "Is she on drugs or something?"

Chris froze like an ice statue, and even Ash was backing away slowly. They'd never had someone threaten to walk out before. The traditions hadn't planned for something like this happening.

A lump formed in Shane's throat. Josh was about to walk out and they were fucked. Dead as a tree in the desert. Shane glanced at his brothers and heaved a sigh. Some things were more important. Somebody had to fix the situation and nobody else was moving a muscle.

"Look, Josh, buddy," he said, putting a hand on Josh's shoulder and hoping for the best. "I know it's not what you were expecting, just think of it as something you can tell ya mates about tomorrow."

"What are you doing, mate?" Chris cried, his face screwed up in disbelief. "Can't you keep your mouth shut for five bloody minutes?"

"I didn't see you doing anything to help. It's not like the ritual won't still go ahead. Would you rather Josh walk out the door?" If Shane was a dragon, his words would have been flaming.

Chris recoiled like Shane had punched him. "What do you think?"

Shane bit his tongue on a snarky comeback, and looked at Josh instead. "How about it, buddy? It'd heaps help us out if you stick around." Josh stared into the distance and thought about it so long the silence became thick enough to cut with a knife. The three Southern elves and their Northern cousins held their breath. Even the Bathtub Bouncers stopped setting up to see what his decision would be.

"What are you doing?" Sovereign Aeria demanded after several long seconds. "Why are we not advancing? Doesn't the human know we have a ritual to complete?"

"Seriously, ya Highness?" Shane snapped, whirling on the sovereign. He was sick of her giving this human shit for no reason. They needed humans to make sure all elfkind didn't die out. "I don't know how ya do things 'round your way, but this is our turf, and our humans. I'm sick of you treating both of us as less than. Give us some respect—'specially after we saved your arse last time."

All the air left the room. Sovereign Aeria opened and closed her mouth several times, no sound coming out. She fiddled with her hands while her lips tightened in annoyance. Shane's heart stopped for a second. Chris was right. Why couldn't he keep his mouth shut?

Then her face changed, she tilted her head, and gazed at Shane.

"What's she doing?" Josh asked, screwing his eyes up.

"How the fuck am I supposed to know," Shane hissed, waiting for the inevitable ear bashing. He was dead meat for sure.

"Few have dared talk to me in such a way," the sovereign said eventually.

Shane's stomach clenched. She was about to berate him for sure.

"You are correct," she carried on, and Shane's jaw hit the floor. "I had no right to conduct myself in the manner in which I did. I am sorry. We had better continue before the night is out."

"Excellent." Chris clasped his hands and faced the room, an overly bright smile on his face. "Every year we gather, our two elven clans, to celebrate the solstice here. Josh, I need you to step in the circle, mate. Try not to smudge the chalk."

Josh looked like a deer in the headlights, but stumbled into the circle anyway. He even managed not to scuff the chalk.

All the tension rushed out of Shane's body. It might still work out alright.

Sovereign Aeria smiled. "Thank you. Your sacrifice will not be forgotten."

"Wait. Nobody said anything about a sacrifice," Josh said, eyebrows bunching in alarm. "I'm not waiting around to get stabbed in the chest."

Sovereign Aeria spluttered, "What gave you the impression that we would do that?"

"Isn't that what sacrifices are? They lay youse down on an altar and stab ya?"

"Nah, not these days," Ash replied. "We used to, but then humans changed, got more civilised."

"We need you to go north and dance with the Midnight King," Chris said.

"North? Like the Sunny Coast? I got family there."

"No, not quite. It is nearer to the Arctic Circle," the sovereign answered.

"Fuck me. Youse are all on drugs. It'll take at least a day to get there. Stuff ya ritual, I'm going home." Josh spun on a heel and stumbled.

Shane groaned. It was going to fall apart there, after everything else that'd happened? This was the Murphy's law of rituals. He really liked the human, and didn't want to see him go. But, Josh was getting narky, and, if he was honest, Shane couldn't blame him. He'd have been sceptical about a ritual involving somewhere on the other side of the planet, too, if he didn't know any better. A faint yellow glow spread through the room. Shane frowned. Was Aeria glowing?

"Fucken hell, somebody slipped me something, I swear," Josh said, shaking his head. "This can't be real."

"It is perfectly real, I assure you," Sovereign Aeria said. Her tone was sharp, but she had a smile on her face. She sighed. "I understand you have had enough, but it is vital we complete the ritual to ensure the continuance of my people."

"It's super important to youse, isn't it?" Josh replied, not taking his eyes off the glow.

"Yes, it is. We cannot risk the wrath of the Midnight King." Aeria's eyes pleaded with Josh, eyes shining in the fairy lights. "Please. Say you will do it."

Josh shrugged. "Fuck it. Why not? But I don't understand why it has to be someone from down here. Can't you lot get someone from round your way?"

"The Midnight King only accepts those with winter in their veins, but he is bound to the North," the sovereign replied.

"Ri-ight. So, why winter? What's so special about it?"

"In times past, we performed the sacrifice once a year on the winter solstice. But in more recent times, it has to be enacted twice a year, so we observe the winter solstice in the Great Southern Land as well."

Josh nodded. "Righto, if it makes ya happy, I'm in."

"Thank you," the sovereign said, throwing her hands in the air.

The band burst into song, a fast beat mixing with pounding guitars and a bassline Shane felt in his gut. Chris'd spent weeks getting the Bathtub Bouncers to play this right, and there was nowhere else he'd rather be, right then. All he needed was a moshpit and the night would be complete.

Shane swallowed past the lump in his throat. This ritual had to go right. He couldn't stand the thought of dying and never feeling that euphoria again.

The sovereign took a step back, her arms flung wide. Seconds later, a string of words in a high, lilting melody flowed from her mouth, weaving through the music. Josh gasped when the chalk glowed and the air shimmered.

The music built up and up until it reached breakneck pace. The drummer's arms were nothing more than a blur.

"Bloody hell," Josh whispered, mouth an 'o' of awe.

It took seconds until the light was too thick to see the human anymore. The singing and music reached a climax then cut off dead in an instant. The light vanished in a blink. The circle was empty again, the air ringing with the absence of any sound.

"Still think somebody should have gone with him. Pretty shithouse how we can't," Shane said, cutting through the silence.

"You know elves cannot enter the Midnight King's domain. We perish if we set foot inside. He must go alone," Sovereign Aeria replied.

"I'm not even sure he's in a fit state to dance. Seriously, the king'll chew him up and spit him out. I like the bloke, but I don't understand how we can put all our lives in Josh's hands when he has no idea what he's doing. What if the king kills him?"

"Of course the elf who keeps breaking tradition would say that," Chris growled.

"Only because everyone else froze up. There's no fucking point me staying quiet if we can't finish the sacrifice, is there? And now, there's a chance Josh won't come back."

"Will you stop thinking of worst case scenarios, mate?" Chris replied. "He'll be fine—"

"How do you know that?" Shane searched Chris's face for answers. Images of imaginary elves blinking out of existence sent Shane's pulse racing like a bullet train. "Seriously, the ritual has never gone like it has tonight. Everything's gone wrong, and no-one's ever even seen what the Midnight King does."

"You are right," Sovereign Aeria intervened, with a small nod. "However, I trust the Midnight King will treat Josh with respect, and the ritual will be completed to our satisfaction."

Shane heaved a sigh. "Fine. I guess I just don't like the idea of packing some random human off to another plane of existence with no warning when it's our lives on the line."

"Come on, buddy," Ash said, trying to calm him down. "Let's grab a drink and crank the music while we're waiting for Josh to come back. Might as well enjoy it."

Shane slumped onto the floor with his back against the stage. Chris handed him a bottle of beer and sat down next to him. The bassist started up a familiar riff and Shane grinned. He took a swig of beer and gazed at the room; so many good memories of all the shows he'd seen there. His brother was right; he was worrying for no reason.

The minutes slipped by. Shane finished his beer, and stood to grab another one when a light blazed through the room from the direction of the chalk circle. The faint sound of bells tinkling sent shivers down Shane's back.

"He didn't last long," he said, quirking his lips.

"It never does, remember?" Ash replied.

Chris waved a hand to shush him as the light dissipated. They peered at the circle, all holding their breath. It was empty.

"What the fuck?" Shane asked, his mouth as dry as the Great Sandy Desert. He should've known better than to relax. "Where's Josh? Didn't I tell ya it was a mistake sending him by himself?" Guilt and fear left a sour taste in his mouth.

"Settle down, mate," Chris replied, tugging at his shirt collar. "There could just be a small delay."

"Settle down? Are you serious?" Worst case scenarios cascaded out of control through his mind. "I don't know about you, but I like being alive. We're responsible for Josh, you know, and he could be stranded on another plane, unable to get back. He doesn't deserve that. Anyway, he's a good bloke—I could maybe go to gigs with him. Seriously, if he's not out in fifteen seconds, I'm going in and grabbing him myself."

"What is wrong with you?" Ash said, his hands spread wide. "Chill the fuck out and have a little patience for fuck's sake."

"Shane, Ash, shut up," Chris snapped. "We should ask Sovereign Aeria before jumping to the worst conclusions."

Shane and Ash stared at their feet. "Yeah, you're right," Shane muttered.

The sovereign nodded. "Ash is correct. There can be a small delay between the light and the human returning, but I will admit—" A biting wind blew in from somewhere, cutting her off.

Shane shivered, then swore. In the middle of the chalk, Josh sat cross-legged, with a dippy grin on his face.

"Whatever you gave me, it was a fucken trip," he exclaimed, swaying from side to side. "There was this bloke with some kinda crown on his head and a cloak. I think the crown was made of bone. It was full on. We did this dance thing where he twirled me around a bit, and there was green lights in the sky. I always wanted to go on Dancing with the Stars—didn't wanna leave."

Shane nearly collapsed from relief.

"Thank the stars!" the sovereign said, her breath coming in quick spurts. "We are saved until the Northern Winter Solstice." She peered at Josh like he was a second thought. "Josh, are you well?"

"Yeah, mate, I'm fucken fantastic. Can I go back? That's the best time I've had since the footy finals two years ago."

"You want to go back?" The sovereign's eyebrows disappeared into her hairline. "There is a first time for everything, I suppose."

"Are you joking? He's a ripper fella, that bloke. Showed me some sick-arse moves."

The sovereign beamed. "I am glad you enjoyed it. Thank you for your help."

"No worries, but I'm serious, could I do this again?"

"See how you feel in the morning," Shane said, dead set sure the human wouldn't remember.

"Morning? You mean I'm not going back?" Josh stuck his bottom lip out.

"Perhaps I could offer a solution," Sovereign Aeria said. "I had my doubts at first, but if young Josh is so keen to offer his services, I am more than happy for him to participate in all future sacrifices."

"Sweet as! I guess I'm pretty tired," Josh said with a loud yawn.

Shane smiled, his cheeks flooding with heat from his earlier hissy fit. They'd live to see another day. He should've known it'd be alright. "Come on, mate," he said. "Let's get you home."

About the Author:

Aussie former music journalist, now working in Payroll and moonlighting as an author. Fantasy and sci fi are hands down her favourite genres, both to read and write after she got the writing bug after reading the Discworld series as a kid, and Sir Terry remains her favourite author of all time. When she's not writing, she loves hanging out with her family watching Star Trek or sport to relax.

Mount Wellington looms over Hobart, 1,271 meters of ancient and unknowable terror.

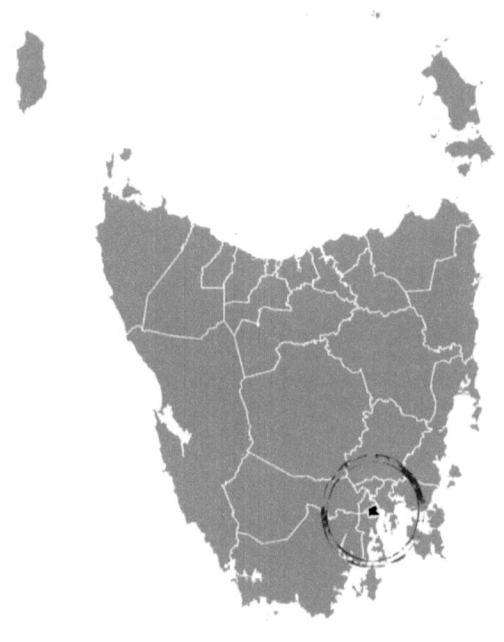

NO PLACE LIKE GNOME

Rachel Nightingale

It is a truth universally concealed that Hobart's Organ Pipes contain unexpected surprises for even the most experienced rock climber. It's an alpine environment but incredibly, it's only 1,000 meters and 20 minutes from downtown Hobart. The dolerite buttresses offer many routes to the summit, each with their own character, but with an overall flavour of 'steep and sustained'. Yet when you look up at *kunanyi* from the city, though the Organ Pipes are visible on one side, the impression is of a smooth, almost dome-like mountain. To see it from a distance gives you no idea of what truly lies in wait for those brave enough to strap on their gear, tape up their hands and use every trick in the book to get to the top.

Having done three (out of some eighty) climbs on The Buttress, I wouldn't consider myself an expert, but it's safe to say I'm hooked. I've been on Circus Wall, where I finished two Grade 17s—*Faith, Hope and Deliverance* and the classic *On the Road Again* as well as the short but strenuous finger cracks and laybacks of Centre Stage (Grade 18). Due to an intense training schedule I've been moving up the grades quickly, though my friends are getting a little bored with me sharing the minutia of every move on the ascents. Last weekend we were sitting outside Knopwoods (known as

Knoppies by locals), the oldest pub in Salamanca enjoying the late spring sunlight. I had my usual Gillespie's in front of me, the alcoholic ginger beer going down a treat, as Chris and I talked about our next trip—I felt ready to tackle *Spartan Ethics*, a 100m Grade 20 on Battlecruiser Ledge. I suppose I was going on a bit, but thought it was kind of rude when Jen snapped.

"Seriously, Gil, can we talk about something else? We've heard this a few times. 'Sheer beauty of nature . . . blah, blah . . . the thrill of a really difficult crux . . . etcetera.' Please, please promise you won't tell us every single detail of your next trip."

The others agreed with her, so Chris and I shrugged our shoulders and promised we'd only give them the highlights . . . the cliff notes, if you like. Little bit of rock-climbing humour there.

Before we started the climb today, I was still annoyed by that conversation. Half the fun of climbing is reliving it when you're safely back on the ground, like watching a movie you gave your soul to film. All the thrills without the risk of spills. But right now, seventy-five metres up the rock face, I've let all that go. There's no room in my mind for negative emotions. Being in the right headspace is everything. Climbing is a mental game as much as a physical one. And when the climb is called *Spartan Ethics*, you can definitely expect challenges in both arenas.

I've reached the crux and have to leave the safety of my small ledge to surmount a bulge to gain a hanging corner. The exposure is intimidating, which feeds my insecurity at leaving the small, comforting tree growing on the ledge. It's not a great practice, but I've popped a sling around the tree just in case the nut pulls from the crack. As is often the case, there is either room for protection *or* a handhold and, well, my hands will just have to find something else. Chris is some 20 metres below, paying out and taking up slack as I gather my courage—one, two moves up and then back down to the ledge. Like a fish on a line . . . Chris calls out from below, encouraging me. The mild spring sun is a comforting blanket on my shoulders.

The next bit's going to be the hardest, and I can almost feel my muscles burning in anticipation. But I'm ready. I take a deep breath. There's a little hold for my left hand just under the bulge, and I move my feet up as far as possible, pulling with my left arm to find a hand jam in the crack rising from the bulge. Seventy-five metres below me is the yellow-green of the sparse native bush. My mind narrows to a single point of focus. Everything depends on this next move.

But I'm in perfect flow, my body and mind meshed. My left forearm is hot and tight, and my feet slip a little as my toes instinctively curl around the edge of the rock. I reach way up, off balance but still on trajectory, rise above the bulge and lock my right hand into the crack, release my left hand, move my weight over the bulge, and mould my left hand into the crack. With the weight change, my feet pop and I'm suspended on the rock face for an eternal moment by two hand jams and my will. Sometimes climbing is half gymnastics. A leap into the unknown. My feet burst into action, coming up to meet my hands over the bulge and I pull down hard, rising a full body length and re-set, stemming into the corner while I puff for breath.

I've done it. I've passed the crux of the climb, the most difficult part. The exhilaration is immense. The first order of business is to find a cam to fit into the crack, my hands shaky as I take it off my harness. I fiddle the cam into place, clip the draw and then my rope, and set a second piece just above the first. There is no way I'm doing that bulge again! Trying to catch my breath, I don't call out, but Chris can be confident I've made it since I haven't landed on top of him. I shake out and take a quick rest before continuing to the top. My breath is still coming fast, loud in my ears, so when there's a grinding like rocks tumbling over each other nearby, I don't register the words at first. Then the sound comes again.

"Nice work, bud. We need to talk."

I whip my head around. Startled doesn't begin to cover it. I'm 75 metres above the ground, wedged in a crack on the side of a mountain. There are still 20 metres of stemming up the corner crack before the end of the climb, and that distance is completely vertical. And the voice is close, not someone calling down at me from above.

"Look left, bud. Look left."

He sounds like Tom Waits, all gravel and whisky. Left of me is the inner edge of the corner. It's a seamless join, two rockfaces meeting at an inward bend.

"And up. That's it. Good lad."

I raise my chin and see that the join ends at a small platform. And standing on that platform is what looks awfully like a garden gnome.

"What the . . ?"

He has green pants, a white shirt and blue vest, and a pointed red hat. And an attitude.

"Take a breath mate, take a breath. We don't want you letting go from shock. It's a long way down. And sometimes bolts that have been drilled into the rocks get a bit slippy, if you know what I mean."

I blink. "Are you . . . threatening me? You're thirty centimetres tall!"

The gnome reaches out a stumpy arm and taps me on the nose. "But the mountain's on my side, see. Now, we need to have words, and it might be easier if you're on stable ground. Can't hold a pen when you're holding on for dear life, eh?"

"A pen? What do I need to hold a pen for?"

The gnome scratches his beard. "I'll explain in a bit. Name's Bob, by the way." He waves his stumpy arm. "Step inside."

The rock my back is pushed into moves, while the one my feet are pressed against shifts the other way, so they splitting apart.

73

"Better grab my arm, lad, before you fall." Bob's little hand reaches for mine.

"You've got to be kidding." Normally I'd laugh at the absurdity of it, but with my secure crevice coming apart around me I'm about to find myself suspended off the side of the mountain by a bolt and some climbing rope, so humour's in short supply.

Bob doesn't respond, just grabs my hand and yanks. He packs a lot of power for a little fella.

I feel myself flying towards him, then everything goes black as the rock face behind me grinds closed. I'm surrounded by a darkness so heavy I can't even see my hands. There's solid ground beneath my feet, and I'm still bent over, but when I try to straighten up my head hits rock.

"Might want to crawl," Bob growls in the darkness. "This way."

"Which way, you little nob?" I might be getting a little bit annoyed.

He chuckles, a sound like rocks being tipped out of a tin. "Sorry, forgot you can't see in the dark. Just crawl forward, you're pointed in the right direction."

The thing is, I've still got my climbing gear attached to me, my harness and rack, and the rope is still attached to both me and the cams I inserted in the crack. There shouldn't be a lot of give. I expect to be pulled short at any moment as I crawl through the darkness. But before that can happen, I bang my forehead into rock.

"Ah, sh—"

"Short overhang here . . . sorry, too late." I swear Bob's laughing.

A burst of anger shoots through me but I let it go. I'm at the little blighter's mercy. But I move forward warily now. No trusting that psychopathic garden gnome anymore. My hand gropes in front of me. There's a wall straight ahead, and a gap to the right, with a faint light in that direction too.

I've just crawled several metres inside the mountain, and should be feeling the pull of my rope now. Fumbling in the dark for my rack, I bump the cams so they jangle against each other, but the rope's gone. Since I'm standing on solid ground, it's not an immediate issue—I'm not about to fall down the mountain—but I'm shaken by its absence. Your rope is your lifeline.

"Looking for that bit of twine, eh?" Bob's voice growls at me from up ahead. "I slipped it off you before we came in. Don't worry, you're safe here. You can tie yourself up again when you head back."

"But where are we going?"

"Just around this corner."

As he finishes speaking there's a grinding sound and the light grows much brighter. Bob runs round the corner he mentioned, his clothes jewel-bright in the flaring light, then he's gone. Manoeuvring myself to follow him is not easy in a space built for gnomes.

A space built for gnomes? There's no such thing. None of this can be real. Did I fall, taking the bulge? Am I lying among the scrub at the bottom of the buttress, concussed, legs smashed to smithereens? But the rock is solid around me, scraping my skin, pushing against my legs. I can stay here, doubting my sanity, or I can take the corner and see what's going on.

I round the bend. There's a circle of radiance up ahead and I crawl towards it. It's a hole slightly larger than my shoulders, and I push my way through, then tumble down a short slope into a cave with several skylights through which bright sunlight streams. And it is *filled* with gnomes, maybe a hundred, all different shapes and sizes. Most are male, but there is the occasional female—I think. There's a riot of colours and patterns in their clothing, although some are cement grey all over, and there are a couple of those weird modern gnomes, all monochrome silver or red. A lot are carrying a shovel or a basket. A few sit astride snails or squirrels. And every single one is staring at me.

"Found another one," Bob growls. The space erupts into a cheer that echoes and bounces.

I'm in a natural circular cave. It's not large enough to stand up in. Dotted all around the edges are arches leading into blackness, similar in size to the one I've just come through. I wonder if they lead to other tunnels, other cliff faces.

A gnome who looks remarkably like Bob, but with a yellow cap, steps forward and jabs a stumpy finger in my knee. "Did you bring us one?" His voice has the same gravel texture.

Bob steps in front of me, the gesture oddly protective. "Don't be stupid, Gary. He hasn't been here before. He doesn't know. Can't you tell? We've never seen him before, have we?"

Gary humphs. "How am I supposed to know? They all look alike to me."

There's a lot of murmuring going on amongst the gnomes, but a whispering sound, like wind through trees, sweeps the room, and they fall silent. A couple of larger gnomes roll something forward through the crowd. It's a female gnome sitting on a mushroom. Her gnome bodyguards have managed to attach little wooden wheels to the stem. With a final grunt, the odd little group comes to a stop in front of me and the mushroom riding gnome speaks.

"Hello! I'm Clarissa." She has long brown braids and a book open in her lap.

"Um . . . nice to meet you?"

"You too. What's your name?"

"I'm Gil."

"Hello Gil. I want to tell you a story."

Since I don't have a lot of choice in the matter, I shuffle around from my crawling position to sit cross legged. My head brushes the ceiling. As I move, there are a few cries of "watch it". I do my best not to bump any gnomes, but there's a plague of them so it's tricky. Finally, I'm seated, and Clarissa begins.

"Once upon a time there was a rock climber. His name was Scott."

"All hail Scott the First, bravest of climbers," the gnomes chant in eerie unison.

"Scott was the first to climb these parts," Clarissa continues, obviously used to the interruptions. "He loved it so much, he returned again and again. And, recognising the might of *kunanyi*, he realised he must bring an offering to the great mountain. So he brought a garden gnome from his home in Sandy Bay."

She waves an arm, and a gnome approaches. He has a number of chips missing from his face and limbs and his paint is faded, leaving only a few dappled swatches of colour. He hobbles close, and gives a stiff bow.

"Name's Bartholomew," the gnome growls.

"An honour to meet you," I say. I offer my hand, but Bartholomew ignores it and shuffles away. I'm not impressed by the manners of gnomes.

Clarissa smiles and continues. "For a few years, Scott and his friend David were the only ones who brought gnomes to the Organ Pipes. They would leave them in places that a very experienced climber could reach, these gifts to the mountain. After a while, other climbers came, and on discovering the hidden gnomes, they too began to follow the tradition. Then one fine day it snowed in

Hobart. The whole city was blanketed in white. And everyone in the town celebrated, taking the day off school or work, having fun in the snow. Their joy was carried up through the icy air, and all the gnomes hidden up here came to life."

She pauses as the gnomes give a great cheer.

"Once we awoke, the great *kunanyi* opened her secret heart to us, creating places within where we could gather and celebrate, until we became the thriving colony we are today."

Another cheer echoes.

"So . . ." Clarissa silences them with a single word. I have the feeling she would slam her book closed if it wasn't made of cement. "It must be obvious to you what we require."

I stare at her blankly. Gary, who's still standing close by, pokes my knee.

Bob mumbles. "Guy's an idiot."

I look around the room at a hundred tiny faces, staring at me expectantly. At last I get it. "You want me to bring you a garden gnome."

"Every time you climb, bud, every time you climb," Bob mutters.

I nod. "Okay."

"There is one other request," Clarissa continues. She holds her hand up and gives it an odd shake. It takes me a moment to realise she's snapping her fingers, but because they're cemented together, it's not working.

Four gnomes come forward carrying a large sheet of paper between them. Another two bring a pen. One of these little guys is a modern silver gnome. As he turns his head, his shiny cheek catches a sunbeam and flashes it into my eye.

"We need you to sign this," Clarissa says. "It's a standard agreement saying you promise not to tell anyone about us."

The words leave my mouth without thought. "What? No! This is the best story ever!"

I love recounting my climbs, and this is the most exciting thing that's ever happened during one.

Clarissa frowns. "No one can know there's a colony of gnomes living on the mountain. Can you imagine the tourists?"

The colourful little blighters take a step towards me, almost as one. There's an immediate shift in the mood of the room . . . um, cavern.

Bob jumps on my leg and runs up to my knee. He glares at me. "Do you remember I told you the mountain's on our side?"

I nod.

"Well, if you don't sign this, you're done. You'll have to find somewhere else to climb, because if you come back here, *kunanyi* will go against you. Every time you turn up with your skinny butt and all your jangly things, you'll be halfway up a cliff face when a crack narrows or widens, or a rock crumbles underfoot . . . always when you least expect it. Not what you need when you're hanging by your fingertips, eh?"

"Bob, Bob, we don't need to threaten him," Clarissa soothes.

"I think we do," the little guy says, and stomps a foot on my kneecap. Other gnomes crowd around and a dozen tiny fingers poke me. It's obvious they all think the same way Bob does. I hold out for a few seconds, not wanting to seem like a bunch of tiny gnomes can intimidate me, but the thought of my cam slipping out of a shifting crack is enough to make me agree. My life depends on those tiny pieces of equipment holding. Not to mention, with all those pointy hats and beards turned in my direction, I'm a tiny bit terrified.

"Okay," I breathe. A wave of cheering rushes across the room as I reach for the pen.

The contract is very straightforward, although it's hard to read such small writing. How on earth they managed to hold a pen to write it, I have no idea. I sign with a flourish. Then a little girl gnome in a pink dress comes forward holding a gumnut full of glistening liquid. Clarissa is holding one of these as well.

"A drink to seal the deal," she says with a smile.

"Just a moment," Bob grumbles. "I wanna have a final word." Clarissa nods permission. Bob runs down my leg and stands on the rock in front of me, waving a tiny fist in my direction.

"Make sure you bring back a girl gnome. There are too many blokes around here. It gets a bit narky sometimes. And we don't want any more of them modern cyborg types." He points the tip of his hat at the silver monochrome gnome, who blushes platinum. "Got it?"

I nod. "Got it."

He gives me what I assume is a rare smile, then steps aside.

Clarissa and I raise our gumnut cups in salute, and throw back our drinks. Though it's barely a drop, as it slides down my throat it's the most refreshing drink I've ever had. Soft as liquid moonlight, sweet as the syrup of a flower, cold as the freshest snow from the peak of *kunanyi*. A strange sensation seeps through my whole body.

When I come to, I hear Chris calling my name.

"Gil? Gil, should I come on up?"

I'm back in the inverted corner, safely attached to my rope. Far below, Hobart is clustered around the undulating river Derwent. Houses are creeping further and further up the mountain, into the wild places, but the peak of *kunanyi* will never be breached, I hope. I feel sorry for anyone who tries.

"Sorry to keep you waiting," I yell down. "I had a bit of a thing."

"What do you mean, waiting? You only went over the bulge half a minute ago."

That makes no sense to me. My limbs are no longer burning from the ascent. I know how my body responds to a climb. Even if I didn't have the memory of spending all that time chatting to a suburb's worth of gnomes and listening to a story, there's no way I could have shaken off my climb burn and fatigue this fast.

"Come on up," I call, and brace myself to take Chris's weight.

I should be spotting him, but for some reason I glance behind me. There's Bob, perched on a platform on top of a crag, just as he was when I first saw him. He's not moving.

"That was a good trick," I say, "getting me back out here."

He doesn't respond.

"It's been fun," I try again. "Even if you are a grumpy little git."

Still he doesn't move.

"Coming over," Chris calls, and I have to turn back and concentrate. There's a tense moment as Chris makes the move, conquering the crux, then he shuffles in beside me.

"Oh look, a garden gnome. What on earth is that doing here?"

* * *

A week later I'm walking along the Hobart waterfront towards Knoppies for a catch up with the mates. The sun is glinting off the Derwent as yachts of all sizes rise and fall on the gentle swell. It's a beautiful day, bright but not too hot. There are tourists everywhere, crowding the outdoor seating of all the pier restaurants, glasses of white wine going down smoothly. Others are walking along the side of the road, taking in the statues and eating cones of what has to be Valhalla ice cream. Enjoying all the delights as the days fade into Hobart's gentle summer.

I catch some of the passers-by looking up at the mountain, blue and majestic in the distance, and think of the secrets concealed in her cracks and crevices, secrets these tourists will never discover.

Did I experience what I remember or was it just some strange adrenaline hallucination?

Someone calls my name. I hear footsteps behind me, then Jen pokes me in the ribs. "Hey, Gil. How's it going?"

"Yeah, good."

We stroll along side by side, chatting. As we reach the grassed area near Salamanca, Jen broaches the topic I've been avoiding.

"So, are you going to tell us all about your latest climb?"

Bob's gravelly voice echoes in my mind. "The mountain's on our side." I shrug with forced nonchalance. "No, I made a promise. I'm not going to say anything."

Jen stares at me. "It was great, we didn't fall. That's all you need to know."

She nods. "Okay. I guess I did ask for that."

I glance up at *kunanyi*. In the shimmering sunlight I almost imagine I can see it breathing. Watching. We cross the cobbled road to Knoppies, and I change the subject, careful to make my question sound like a completely new topic. "Hey, do you have any idea where I can buy a garden gnome?"

* No garden gnomes were harmed in the making of this story.

About the Author:

Rachel Nightingale is an author, award-winning playwright, educator and actor. With a passion for storytelling and the theatre, it was only natural that her first fantasy series, the *Tales of Tarya* trilogy, would centre on both. She has also co-authored *Mandala: Journeys Within the Circle*, with artist Karen Scott. Having survived improv theatre, travelled the world and immersed herself endlessly in research and creative practice, she often finds herself at the mercy of stories that demand to be written. She lives in regional Australia with her family, a very bossy cat and the cutest dog in the world.

The Pacific Highway on the New South Wales MidCoast is a stretch of road that fills one with a strange sense of familiarity and foreboding.

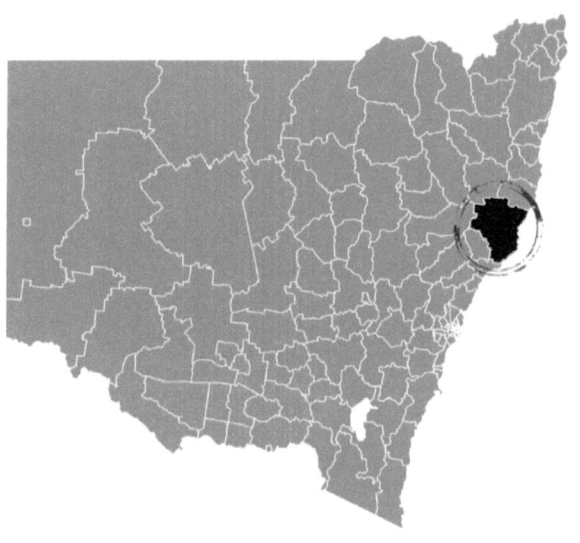

SEA MIST SHORE WITCH

Mikhaeyla Kopievsky

There is a stretch of road that runs twenty kilometres from the sleepy coastal town of Hawks Nest all the way to Bombah. It runs like a dark grey scar, barely wide enough for two lanes of traffic, its edges bleeding into the sandy shoulders and messy scrub of sea grasses. Eucalypts tower along each side like sentinels, flanked by a motley cadre of tea tree and lantana, all of them guarding the Myall River to the west and the Pacific Ocean to east.

Five kilometres in, the towering eucalypts stop abruptly and the flattened landscape sheds its messy understorey. The road runs as straight as a compass needle, surrounded by a forest of banksia trees and a sky that opens up like a blossom to the sun.

Except there is no sun now. And no cars but mine. It is just me, the Hunter's Moon, and the sea mist.

The midnight sky shines bright in the glow of October's full moon. Even with the car windows down, humidity clings to the bare skin of my arms, and the air is so thick with salt, my tongue sings with the taste of it. In the sea mist the finer details of the banksias are obscured; their already-twisted bodies settle into a tangle of trunks and limbs that writhe and dance along the roadside. And in the warm, salty air, echoes the deep-throated growling and mournful howling of the local dingoes.

I grip the steering wheel tighter and pull the car over onto a sandy embankment. It is the sign I've been waiting for—the one that tells me the Shore Witch is near.

* * *

Not far from the Mungo Brush coast, languishing just above the thirty-second parallel, sits Broughton Island. On this windswept outcrop, where sea grasses flail like whips in the unrelenting southerlies, a cluster of fishermen's shacks squat low against the hill. Built in the 1930s, their timber is warped and whitewashed, and the solar panels and rainwater tanks of more recent decades sit rusted and shattered. Once, they attracted intrepid adventurers and daytripping sailors—wildfinders escaping reality into a world that was raw and unbridled and isolated. Now they shelter only ghosts, their broken lintels adorned with oyster shells and the wishbones torn from wedge-tailed shearwater birds who still brave the island's ravages to mate and nest.

The power of the Shore Witch is strong here; a single whisper from her salt-cracked lips is enough to cleave the cliffs in two and drag storm clouds across the sky like caul fat.

The legends have called her many names—Garrawerrigali, Czarny Królik, Jimmy's Mistress—but now she is known by the name that is immortalised in the maps of her birthplace: Esmerelda. The name schoolchildren sing as they jump rope in the playground.

Esmerelda of the isle,

her blood so black, her face so vile.

Esmeralda of the shore,

will break your bones, then break some more.

How many bones will she break?

How many children will she take?

One, two, three, four . . .

* * *

My bare feet crush the spiky grasses of the undergrowth, toes sinking into sand kept damp with the rising tide. There are rules when seeking the Shore Witch, and no shoes is one of them. On my left foot is the symbol for *arriving*: four concentric circles pierced with four lines on each side, drawn crudely with black permanent marker. On my right the symbol for *returning*: an arc with five radiating lines like a rising sun. The first symbol to find the witch, the second to find my way back.

I close my eyes. The smell of salt sings bolder and the sound of nearby waves roars louder. My steps are hesitant, the fear bubbling in my chest keeping tempo with the skipping song I hum under my breath.

Branches of banksia trees scratch at my arms, but I keep my eyes closed and my feet moving. In my self-imposed blindness, it is easy to imagine the limbs as the bony fingers of the Shore Witch, prodding at my flesh, finding the ripe parts, testing for tenderness.

My skin crawls with the thought of it, but I keep moving and the branches keep scratching.

"Your heart is brave, but your feet are not," the voice drifts in the air—not the harsh rasp I was expecting, but something younger and softer. "Open your eyes, child—show me your gifts of payment."

I do as she says. Her hair flows like the kelp forests off the eastern shores of Broughton Island, her skin unlined and translucent like pearl nacre. She fixes her turquoise eyes on me, her hand outstretched and palm open.

My fingers are calm, despite the tremors in my chest, as I pull three small objects from my satchel. *Blood on a memory, timber etched with bone, the hair of a loved one wrapped twice 'round a stone.* The cost of entreaty, payment for the Shore Witch to hear my plea. She snatches them greedily and turns them over in her hand, appraising each one in turn: a polaroid of my mother, the faded colours dating it as much as the 70s fashion, its white edge marred by old blood where I'd pressed my pinpricked thumb to the glossy paper; my favourite sketching pencil sharpened with the filed-down bone shard of a possum carcass left on Waynderrabah Beach; and the lock of hair from my sister's first haircut, raided from my mother's keepsake chest and wrapped around a river pebble ground smooth by the persistence of the Myall River. All three were as precious and useless as any random collection of inanimate objects, and all three looked as if they had always belonged to the witch.

"They are acceptable," she says, her voice an echo of the waves tumbling beyond the sand hills. She tucks the objects into the folds of her dress, where they disappear behind a patchwork of sails cut from ships wrecked on the rocks off the island. "I will hear your plea."

Bathed in silver light and caught in the gaze of the Shore Witch, I pull together every shred of courage lurking at the dark edges of my heart and press them into a tight ball of fire. "I want my sister back."

The Shore Witch smiles at me, her dress swirling around her feet like sea water eddying in a tidal pool. Low-throated growls rumble in the distance. She presses salt-kissed palms to my cheeks, turquoise eyes rolling back into her head and leaving behind milky globes. "The price is high for returning a dingo girl," she murmurs.

I look to the south, the sound of hunting dingoes drawing closer. "I'm ready to pay."

* * *

It hadn't happened suddenly—no flicking of a light switch, no erratic shift from one personality to another. Leila's change had been glacial. She'd cried like everyone else had beside Mum's hospital bed, and raged in the weeks afterwards. But then came the silence and the locked bedroom door and the stillness.

Something dark had bloomed inside my sister, its twisted roots wrapping around her heart and stealing her light.

That summer she visited me only twice in my bedroom, when the walls between our rooms seemed paper thin and my sobs kept her from sleep. In those moments she would talk of getting Mum back, her voice tinged with a mania my own grief-drenched mind was deaf to. It was only after she disappeared that I saw how far that mania had developed—her room full of hiding places that held sketches and notes and stories of the Shore Witch.

And then, a year after she left, the mania caught me.

* * *

Thousands of tiny mollusc shells lie scattered on the beach and crunch underfoot as the Shore Witch leads me to the water line. She whistles a low and chaotic tune, bringing six dingoes trotting out from the scrubland.

"Many women have come before you, to petition for power, and riches, and love that doesn't belong to them. Those pleas are easy to grant, and the barbs in their tails obvious. Selfish hearts and simple minds." The dingoes prowl around her, leaving shallow footprints in the wet sand. "But breaking a Hunter's Moon curse . . . that is not easy. Few have tried, most have failed." She tilts her head and peers at me. "Only those who are worthy can break the curse. And those who aren't lose more than their hope when they fail."

I'm not worthy—I'm not strong, or brilliant, or particularly brave. As the younger sister, I was never expected to be; that was always Leila's domain. I'm just the only one who is here and the only one who loves her enough to want her back.

"What do I need to do?"

The Shore Witch smiles, her teeth small and white like miniature conch shells. She turns to the ocean and points to Broughton Island, its uneven landform an ancient giant hulking down in the water. "The contract payment cannot be paid here," she says, her voice a rustling of sea grasses. "To break a Hunter's Moon curse, you must become the hunter. Bring me the still-beating heart of a young cormorant before the sky turns blue, and you shall be gifted the power to break the curse."

She turns to me and presses her fingers to my forehead, murmuring a string of words like forgotten lyrics to an ancient song. The midnight world spins around us, stars stretching into thin ribbons that press closer and wrap us up.

One moment we are standing on the shore, our feet damp in the low-tide sand; the next we are standing on the rocky outcrops of Providence Point and staring back over the water at the mainland. A lone dingo pads in tight, languid circles around the Shore Witch.

"She'll help navigate the island and track the cormorants." The witch buries her fingers into the dingo's tawny fur, bending to murmur something into ears that prick up straight. As she

93

continues to murmur, the dingo begins to tremble—a subtle tremor of frisson traveling along its spine and rippling its fur like a stone dropped in still waters; and then, as the witch's voice grows louder and more sonorous, a violent shaking, like the animal is trapped in an invisible cyclone made only for it.

I clench my eyes shut, fighting against the rising panic, and, when I open them, the dingo is gone. A girl, no older than fifteen, stands next to the witch, her hair the golden colour of dingo fur, eyes sharp and skittish. Like the witch, she is draped in the sun-bleached canvas of shipwreck sails, the fabric adorned with oyster shells and flax flowers stitched with fishing line.

The dingo girl cocks her head at me. "Why does she just stand there?" Her voice is low and gravelly, raising gooseflesh along my arms.

"She will not harm you while she is in this form," the witch says to me, ignoring the dingo girl's question. "But, if you fail to bring me the cormorant heart before morning has settled into the sky, she will revert to her dingo form and devour you."

* * *

The track that runs along the western side of the island takes us over low-lying scrubland and tangles of thick coastal grasses. Once it would have been well-maintained, or trampled down by the boots of tourists and ecologists; but now, after decades of isolation, nature has regained its dominance and removed it of clean lines and sharp angles.

I watch the dingo girl as she moves sure-footed over the knotted landscape, head bent low as if following a scent, tawny hair floating in the breeze that drifts in from the south. I turn my head towards the mainland, picturing the other dingoes that roam the shoreline, wondering whether Leila roams with them.

"How long . . ." My voice falls away, lost in the wind.

"You are too timid to be a hunter," the girl growls. She stops at a thicket of matrush, crouching to push aside the long, spiky leaves that glisten in the moonlight.

"Do you know Leila?" I ask.

"Your dingo girl?" She stands up and shakes her head. "We shed our human names when we transform. What did she petition Aunty for?"

I ignore her question and ask one of my own. "Do you transform often?"

The dingo girl laughs, a deep-throated rumbling, and pads away from the overgrown track. "Forget it. It's not a regular thing. There are hundreds of us, and Aunty only picks one for the black bird hunts. The contract is the only way to break the curse."

She sets off across the ridge. I follow closely, my ink-stained feet stumbling on loose rocks, the skin of my calves suffering a thousand slashes from spears of tall, reedy grass. A thin sheen of sweat catches in the sea breeze and pulls a chill along my spine. Despite the silence of our hunt, the air is a symphony of bird calls—from the resonant gurgles of eastern reef egrets to the tremulous brrrrs of little terns. And everywhere, a salty mist hovers, coating the island in a dream.

"You are too noisy to be a hunter." The dingo girl scowls at me and taps her foot impatiently as I scramble down the shallow cliff behind her to the beach of Coal Shaft Bay. "I don't know why Aunty thought you were worthy."

Because I'm not, I think to myself. *Just determined.* "Why do you call her 'Aunty'? Aren't you angry she cursed you?"

My feet tingle with relief as they leave behind the rocky crag and touch down on soft, cool, damp sand. I look over to the girl and find her fixing me with a curious frown. "We call her Aunty as a sign of respect—she carries a heavier burden than us; her curse is more terrible. She didn't curse me, the one that came before her did."

"The one before?"

She laughs again, her lips pulled back in an almost-snarl. "All curses can be broken. Hers is broken when she finds another to take her place."

"Who would take her place?"

Her golden eyes flash in the moonlight as she turns from me and scans the beach. "Those who fail to meet the Hunter's contract."

* * *

Our feet track deep prints along the beach as the dingo girl stalks towards the northern end where boulders sit like demon's marbles scattered on the shore. Through the haze, they seem to shatter, haphazard pieces lifting away and floating upwards.

The dingo girl growls under her breath and spins around to stare at me. "I thought you wanted to hunt a black bird, not scare them all away."

I look back to the rocks and to the siege of cormorants and shearwaters hovering above them. "What did you petition the Shore Witch for?"

"Questions, questions! You ask too many questions. You *talk* too much. Your mind is too messy. Hunters should be soft and stealthy, but you are all heavy footfalls and clumsy words. Why didn't you ask these questions before you agreed to the contract?"

I turn away from her and burrow my toes into the sand.

"We shed more than our names when we transform," she says, pivoting away from the rocks and moving back towards the cliff. "We shed our memories as well. We don't remember our petitions; we only know they were granted and that our transformation is the payment."

"No, that's not right," I shout after her, sending the birds squawking and flying higher.

"What is not right?" she growls back.

"My sister's petition wasn't granted." Time didn't turn back; Mum was still dead.

She laughs, a soft howl in the night. "If she's a dingo girl, it was granted. Maybe you just don't know what she petitioned."

97

* * *

The walk to Esmerelda Cove is long and disconsolate. The dingo girl covers the distance without looking back at me and I don't ask her any more questions. Ahead, the dark and broken silhouettes of the weathered fishing shacks sit shrouded in sea mist. To my tired eyes, they look like the hulls of great ships torn apart by the craggy fingers of the island's southern reaches and tossed haphazardly to its wrist.

"The birds are too crazed for us to hunt," the girl said. "We'll shelter in one of the huts until they have forgotten us."

"But the witch—"

"Is on the mainland. As she always is on the full moon. Why do you fret on her? She has judged you worthy. She will not move against you unless it is morning and you have failed to meet your part of the contract."

I blink at the girl. The mist is stronger on this part of the island, and if not for the braided heat in my calves and the sharp air pricking in my lungs, I would think it all a dream; but the girl seems different—her gait not as languid, her posture no longer bowed, her voice softer and sweeter and altogether more human.

She drifts towards the shack, passing through the void of its doorway like a wraith into shadows. A whistling builds in the air and sings across the landscape, as if the land itself has cracked and the pressure imprisoned for centuries under the heavy fist of the ocean has found its way into the world.

In the whistling I hear voices—the groaning of old men, the wailing of orphans. I escape from them into the shack.

"You may sleep, if you like." The girl sits cross-legged against the cracked timber boards.

"So you may eat me when the morning comes and I have no cormorant heart to gift the witch?"

The girl laughs, no longer the soft, deep growl, but a tinkling of sea glass on gravestones. "I can not devour you, until the witch gives me permission. And even then I may refuse the pleasure."

I sink to the boards and stretch out my tired legs, keeping my eyes on the girl, but feeling them droop. "Why would you refuse?"

She smiles at me, her wolfish grin returned. "Hunters can be many things: some are fast, where others are strong; some kill their prey quickly, others devour like a slow-burning desire. Some are fierce, some are terrible. But all can show mercy."

* * *

I doze in the strange limbo between sleep and waking. The Shore Witch visits me, her silver hair floating around her face like feathers, and with her are all the Shore Witches of centuries past. They line up behind her, their backs to the one they freed from the curse, their eyes on the one they condemned. They are all stooped, hunched over and burdened with their failure to meet the Hunter's Moon contract.

My Shore Witch crouches down on her haunches and pokes slender fingers into the fleshy part under my eyes, pressing as if to indent the bone beneath and brand it. She whispers to me in the hissing and whistling of the sea, "Open your eyes."

Her fingers curl into bony fists and she raps them on my breastbone. "Open your heart."

Then her hands are at my shoulders; pinching, gripping, shaking.

"Wake up, Hunter. It is nearly morning and you must find your heart." The voice is not the Shore Witch's.

I open my eyes. The dingo girl drops her grip on my collarbone and stands up, silhouetted against the moonlight that filters in through the gaps between the timbers. "This time you must be quieter and faster. The black bird will not wait for you to hunt her young."

* * *

I follow the girl silently as she tracks back to the beach of Coal Shaft Bay, its white sand punctuated with black boulders. The mist is lighter now, but dark clouds have drifted across the moon, and in the moving shadows the sand seems to writhe.

Before I follow the girl down the cliff, I look over to where the cormorants are nesting, and think of all the women that have tried before me to fulfil this contract, and failed. Of all the Shore Witches that cursed the one that followed them.

I imagine them scaling the rocks with their own dingo girl, stalking in the shadows towards the gentler crop of rocks where mother birds nuzzle with their young in a colder and less forgiving nursery. And there my imagination falters.

How do you catch a juvenile cormorant? How do you kill it in a way that keeps its heart beating long enough to meet the terms of the contract? My chest grows tight with the thought that the other women failed because the trial itself is impossible.

Jagged edges tear at my palms as I slip the rest of the way down the cliff, landing with a jolt in the cold sea water lapping at the base. The girl flashes a dark look over her shoulder, but my indiscretion is a minor one and she shifts her glittering eyes away from me and back to the northern shore.

I catch up to her and we stand shoulder-to-shoulder, bare feet sinking into sodden sand, backs to the mainland, eyes to the craggy silhouette ahead.

"Well," she murmurs to me, "what are you waiting for Hunter? Go get your heart."

Dark wings flutter in the pre-dawn sky, flights of seabirds lifting up and hovering in the morning chill, gurgling and cawing as they float back down to the rocks.

"I'm not a Hunter. I don't know how to."

"Learn or try. That, or be a Shore Witch."

* * *

There is a moment, as I creep closer to the rookery, when I think I might be able to do it—to get close enough, to stay hidden in the shadows, to grab one of the young birds. The musty smell of guano dominates the salty air and the steam from warm bodies tangles in the remnant sea mist.

Up close, the cormorants are terrifying and majestic. Perched on rocks like angels of prophecy, they stretch out their dark wings and tilt their heads up, black and bronze feathers fluttering in a silent communication with the island's spirits.

The high-tide waters bury my feet to the ankles. I move slowly, feeling the sand clutch desperately at my bare feet as I lift them out, and just as desperately as I step back down. Clutch, resist, step, clutch, resist, step.

My foot catches on something sharp below the surface, slicing at the skin and opening the wound to the onslaught of salt water. I cry out in a primal moment of reflex, and the birds launch into the air like an overture to the apocalypse.

In a final act of desperation, I lunge forward. My forearms and wrists crash against the rocky outcrop, but incredibly my fingers plunge into feather and clutch around a warm, soft body.

A cloud of cormorants screech above me, the rocks deserted save the bird in my grasp and the one that has drawn itself to full height in front of me. My prisoner squeals and nips at my hands, but the one who watches over it regards me calmly.

The maelstrom around me disappears—reality reduced to the space between my hands and two dark, beady eyes.

I can't do it. I can't snap the elegant, elongated neck; can't pinch tight the pincers of the tiny beak and barricade it from the air; can't sink my fingers in deeper and snap open the fragile ribcage.

I loosen my grip and reality's horizon widens; the bird scampers from my grip, tripping over itself in its haste to bury its head into the breast of its protector, and I shiver as the cold water—now around my hips—seeps into my bones. Slowly I stand up. The protector startles, wrapping a wing around the younger bird and nudging it to flight. Moonlight sneaks through racing clouds and dances on my skin. I shiver again, left in the wake of the rookery now cold and still and empty.

But not completely empty. Left behind in a small crevice between the boulders that have crashed and settled against one another is a young cormorant, its wing broken and breast bloodied. The chaos that had erupted just moments before has left it battered and abandoned; for this one there is no protector, no saviour, no witness.

I move carefully towards it, my chest tightening at the sight of it cowering and shivering. My hands are surer now, they wrap around the tiny body and grip it tightly. Despite the thrumming of blood in my ears, and despite the small and vulnerable frame in my grasp, I can feel its pulse—a rippling against my fingers as the tiny heart beneath, no bigger than my thumb, skitters with the most primal fear of all.

I lift the bird from the crevice and pull it close to my chest, tucking it into the groove above my collar bone.

"What now, Hunter?" The dingo girl's voice drifts to me.

"Take me to the Shore Witch."

"But you must fulfil your part of the contract."

I turn to her. She stands a few feet from me, the moon now low on the horizon and the sky ink fading in the dawn twilight.

"Even Hunters can show mercy. And the contract was for a still-beating heart."

* * *

At the southern-most tip of Esmerelda Cove, with my cormorant chick still pressed against my chest and fluttering nervously, the dingo girl lifts her head to the dawn sky and pierces the silence with a deep howl.

As the sound reverberates against the cliffs and is swallowed by the ocean, the world blinks out of existence for the briefest heartbeat and, when it returns, deposits us onto the mainland.

Amongst the banksias and spear grasses, the Shore Witch emerges. In the lightening sky, she looks less fearsome and more fragile.

"You have brought me the still-beating heart of the great cormorant," she says, her face showing neither surprise nor dissatisfaction. She saunters closer, her dress flowing around her like foam on a wave. The dingo girl pads around her in wide circles, returned to her wild form. The witch ignores her, eyes only on the cormorant chick.

I cradle the bird protectively. "What will you do with it?"

"Nothing you have not done yourself."

She stretches her kelp-kissed fingers to the bird in my grasp, runs them over its dark feathers. The bird squirms against the touch, burrowing deeper against my skin and nipping at my collarbone that juts forward with tension.

I turn my body from the witch, trying to shield the bird, but it thrashes in my hands, its beak pinching my skin so angrily that my grip falters. The chick drops from my grasp and I lunge to recover it, but it simply unfurls its wings and alights into the air, hovering for the briefest of seconds—as if surprised by the sudden freedom—and then sets off east towards the island.

I look back at the witch, her gaze tracking the bird as it crests over the calm waves. "You healed it?" The words come through chattering teeth; my cold, wet body has descended into tremors.

She smiles, small and sad. "Even Hunters can show mercy." She presses her fingers to my forehead and my trembling stops, the cold and damp wicked away so suddenly I doubt they were ever there. Her eyes are guarded when she peers into my own, her head cocked to one side. "Now, to honour your contract."

"Why honour this one, when you did not honour my sister's?" I ask quietly.

"The dingo girl?" She shakes her head. "There are no contracts with dingo girls."

"I don't understand. I thought it was part of the exchange—you grant their petitions, they transform into dingoes."

The dingo at her feet stands alert, golden eyes blinking in the coming morning.

"Many girls petition me to grant their desires. Some are easy: the lost phone number of an ex-lover, a flatter nose or smaller hips, a promotion above their rivals. Some are harder: love they have not earned, power they have not earned, money they have not earned. And some are impossible. A life that is lost cannot be regained; it is not like pulling a fish from the ocean, or knitting together broken bones. For those girls, who come to me full of grief and guilt and despair and emptiness, I offer only a small mercy—I cannot return their departed, but I can take away their misery."

More dingoes pad along the beach to the Shore Witch, golden fur rippling as they stalk across the soft, sodden sand. I search among them for one that could be Leila, looking for something reminiscent of the sister I used to know. But it is hard to remember her without remembering the dark, empty shell she had become before disappearing. The Leila who blamed herself for Mum's death. The Leila who had stayed out past curfew and found herself stranded; who had called Mum to pick her up that dark, rainy night; who had sat huddled in a bus shelter three blocks from where our family's grey sedan had skidded off the road and into cluster of ancient eucalypts.

"You have met your end of the bargain," the witch says, pulling my attention back to her. "I will honour mine. Speak your petition to remove the magic, and it shall be done."

"It will be over? The curse removed?"

"Destroyed like the sea mist when the sun appears."

I open my mouth to speak the words, and falter. I imagine my sister standing where I stand now, and see her as I had in the days before she disappeared: defeated and desperate, her heart hollow, her mind broken. I hear the truth of the Shore Witch's words, they worm their way into my chest and settle heavy against my ribs: there are no contracts with dingo girls, no trials, no trades. Leila's transformation hadn't been the price, but the thing petitioned for.

The wind picks up and a lone dingo emits a solemn growl. I stare down at my feet inked with the runes of finding and returning, the dark lines blurring as salty tears prick my eyes. I had come here to free my sister from the clutches of the Shore Witch, only to find her freed from something much worse: a grief she did not deserve and a guilt she could not live with.

The magic that had bound my sister, that binds her still, was not a curse but a kindness.

"Speak your petition, child. The dawn grows near."

107

I look up at the witch. In her eyes I see the legacy of all the Shore Witches that have come before, and I feel their power radiating from her translucent skin. What had she petitioned for all those years ago? What had been the price of her failure? Had she failed her trial because she had killed the cormorant and stilled its heart? Or because she had been unable to strike a blow?

I touch the skin at my collarbone, still warm where my own cormorant had nestled. *Even Hunters can show mercy.* "The petition will break the Hunter's Moon curse?"

The witch nods. "For your chosen, and her alone."

As the dawn light crests over the horizon, I cast one last glance over the dingoes that surround us, and speak the words to destroy a bond. They drag across my tongue like rusted fishing hooks; a mercy to a stranger and farewell to a sister. "I petition to end the curse of the Shore Witch."

About the Author

Mikhaeyla Kopievsky is an Australian speculative fiction writer and author of the *Divided Elements* series and *Tasmanian Gothic*. Her short stories have been longlisted for the EJ Brady Prize and published in Etherea Magazine and Deadset Press anthologies. Her debut novel, *Resistance*, was a semi-finalist in Hugh Howey's inaugural SPSF Competition and winner of a OneBookTwo Standout Award.

Born in Sydney, Mikhaeyla now lives in the Hunter Valley on Worimi land with her husband, son, two rescue dogs, four Australorp chooks, a hive of cantankerous bees, and the occasional herd of beautiful Black Angus steers. When she is not writing or reading, Mikhaeyla enjoys cooking with the produce harvested from her kitchen garden, going to the beach, stargazing, and training to be a ninja.

W: www.mikhaeylakopievsky.com.
F: https://www.facebook.com/MikhaeylaKopievsky.
T: https://twitter.com/MikhaeylaK.

The Warrumbungle Shire is an easy place to get lost.
It is also the last place you'd want to get lost in.

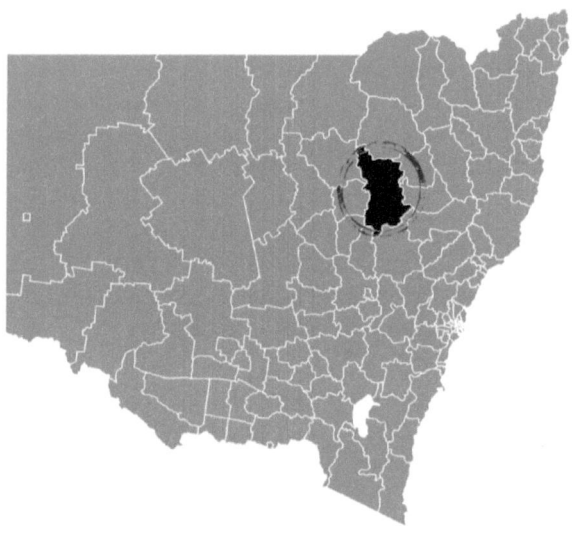

RAIN DANCE

Erin Munzenberger

The sheep lay on its side, its agonised cries hanging in air thick with red dust. Maggots writhed on its exposed flesh. The smell of death and rot rose from its wool like smoke.

A blast of my shotgun put an end to the sheep's screaming, but not to the maggots' ravaging.

The sun beat down, crisping my skin, as I seized the now-dead sheep by a leg and dragged it to the rubbish heap. Sweat trickled down the back of my neck as I hauled. The body was heavy, even though the sheep had been a scrawny thing. The remnants of its flock watched me with wide, slotted eyes from across the dust-bowl paddock. Thin and ragged, there were far too few of them left. The one bumping across the dirt behind me wasn't the first to succumb to fly strike, or to starvation, or the never-ending heat.

A weathered sign beside the shed bore the legend: "Welcome to Red's Farm."

Crows were landing as I tossed the corpse then turned and walked away. I returned to the task that had brought me to the paddock in the first place—trying to fill the trough with water. A faint greasy film was all that remained on the concrete bottom. I turned on the tap and listened to the pipes groan and clang as they struggled to carry water that wasn't there. Hard bubbles of air rattled out, along with the occasional spray of mud, before the tap dribbled a thin red-brown stream.

Hip cocked, I looked back at the sheep—and saw *her* watching me.

Her sun-baked skin was the same red brown as the dust, as the trickle of water oozing out of the tap. Bony arms hung long and thin at *her* sides. Lank hair, the colour of bleached bone, hung from *her* head. *Her* eyes gleamed like those of a fox in the night.

I blinked, and *she* was gone.

* * *

I'd long since given up on trying to keep the dust out of the house. A layer of red coated every surface and tinted the light that battled its way through the windows. Empty brown bottles covered the table and counter tops, a few of them spilling onto the kitchen floor. The remnants of one crunched beneath my boots as I crossed the kitchen, waving away the flies that struggled in drooping circles around my head.

The old spring bed creaked as my weight settled onto it. The mattress smelled of stale sweat. There was a spider on the ceiling the size of my hand, its long legs bent.

A rattle of breath in my ear told me *she* was lying on the bed beside me.

"Please," I said, my voice heavy. "It's barely been a month. I can't keep doing this."

On the ceiling, the spider twitched. One leg snapped, folded over on itself by an invisible hand. The spider tried to run, but it was too late. One by one the rest of its legs were broken or pulled from its body. It squirmed, pinned to the ceiling. Its tiny eyes flickered on its mandibled face.

Was it terrified? Was its spider life flashing before its six spider eyes, a succession of dead bugs and treks across wooden surfaces? I doubted it, and yet I felt its eyes were boring into mine, begging me, *pleading* with me for help.

"All right," I said, defeated. "All right, I'll do it."

The gasping breath beside me stopped. The broken spider peeled off the ceiling and fell with a soft thump to the floor. Its body rocked twice, what was left of its mutilated legs curling over.

"I'll do it," I whispered.

* * *

The old ceiling fan circled overhead, letting off a metallic scrape with each rotation. The tiny pub smelled of old fryer oil, cheap beer and cigarettes. Threadbare carpet stuck to my boots with every step. I claimed a stool at the bar and ordered a Tooheys. My eyes roved over the grizzled regulars—weather-beaten old men with dirt ground into the creases of their faces. Not the sort of fare *she* was looking for. I was pondering my options, whether I would have to make the long drive into a tourist-stop town like Coonabarabran to hunt the caravan parks, when the door of the pub opened and a man and woman walked in, their arms around each other.

They looked young, and foreign—their skin smooth and unweathered, not leathered by the harsh Australian sun. He was tall and red-haired, his eyes hidden behind flash looking sunglasses. She was a vision in khaki shorts, all long, lithe legs, her blonde hair plaited back out of her face.

Bingo.

From my seat at the bar, I had a view of the car park, where a combi van painted like Picasso's vomit the morning after a night on the piss was parked. I set down my empty glass and made my way past the lovebirds, who were now at the bar, making small talk with the barman about their visit to the Siding Spring Observatory. Outside the pub, I leaned against the combi and made a show of lighting a ciggie. My eyes darted all around, making sure I wasn't being watched. When I was certain I was unobserved I pulled the small Stanley knife from my pocket and stabbed it into the back tyre. Just a small cut.

I returned to my own dust-streaked land rover and waited.

* * *

The car park was empty when my quarry emerged from the pub, his arm around her shoulders. As they stopped to kiss and canoodle, my fingers tapped on the steering wheel. At long last, they got into the combi. The van rumbled to life and left the car park.

I waited until it was just at the edge of sight, before following with my headlights off.

Whichever of them was driving, they weren't confident on the rutted dirt track roads. I drummed my fingers on the wheel again as they navigated a series of potholes. They were going far slower than I had anticipated. At this rate, they weren't going to make it far from the pub before the tyre went flat.

A rattling breath over the growl of the land rover's engine. *She* was there, in the corner of my eye.

"You don't need to check up on me," I muttered.

A kangaroo bounded out of the scrub in front of the combi. The sound of fifty odd kilos of skippy connecting with the van's windscreen was horrific—the screaming of animal and metal and the shattering of glass. The driver lost control. Brake lights flared in the night and the combi went clattering off the road through the brush.

"Fucking hell," I snarled, ramming the land rover into park where the combi had plunged off the road. *She* watched as I slammed my way out of the car and stomped into the scrub.

The combi had fetched up against a rock, its front end all crumpled. The couple climbed out, him holding his head, her rubbing her chest where the seat belt and caught her.

"You two alright?" I asked, playing the role of a concerned fellow motorist.

"Jawohl," the blonde muttered, her eyes wide in shock. "Ich glaube schon—I mean, sorry, I think so." She reached for her boyfriend, who was bleeding from a cut above his eye.

"Gotta watch out for them roos." I grabbed the man by the elbow, pulled him along. He didn't resist, placid as a child. "Let me give you a lift. We can get ya car sorted from my place."

"I—" The woman was reluctant to come with me, this total stranger who'd popped out of the bush, but her man was hurt, and the combi wasn't going anywhere anytime soon.

"All right," she said. "Thank you."

"No worries," I herded the pair of them back to the land rover and bundled them into the back. *She* was still in the passenger seat as I climbed behind the wheel, but the couple didn't see her.

* * *

The two Germans were dozing in the back seat as the land rover nosed over the cattle grate and through the home paddock up towards the house.

The blonde woman awoke with a sleepy noise as I pulled the car to a stop. "Wo- where are we?"

"Just at my place," I said. As she shook her boyfriend awake, I walked around to the boot and retrieved my shotgun. It was heavier than usual, its slick and shiny surface greasy against my hands. My boots echoed like gunshots as I crunched over the hard ground, then yanked open the land rover door.

The harsh yellow of the interior light gleamed on the shotgun as I pointed it at the couple. The colour drained from the woman's face, and her fists clenched in her boyfriend's shirt. He stared at me with muzzy eyes. The crash had done more damage to him than I'd realised.

"Out," I barked, gesturing with the gun. They slid out of the car, the blonde steering her man, her face bone-white in the darkness.

"Walk."

The sheep milled in their pen in the shed, perfuming the night with their rank animal musk. Distorted shadows danced against the corrugated iron walls, thrown by the lone flood light hanging from a post. I marched the two of them into the middle of the shit-strewn floor. She wept as he looked around, aimless and confused.

"On ya knees," I growled, dragging over a rusted metal trough, which scraped across the concrete.

"Please," the woman sobbed.

She was there, watching from the shadows, her feral eyes gleaming. For a moment I considered telling the blonde to grab her man and run. I could hold *her* off somehow . . . hell, maybe I could off myself for *her,* the only way left I had to spit in the old bitch's face. I revelled in the fantasy for a moment, imagining the feel of the knife against my throat, my hot blood pumping, and that grizzled visage cracking with surprise, with anger, her clawed hands reaching for me as she sneered, but I would be free of her . . .

A deep sigh escaped me. Who was I kidding? There was no way to be free of her. The day I kicked the bucket was the day I would join the old hag in her miserable half-life, bet my hat on it.

And besides—if I died, who would look after the sheep?

117

"Sorry," I muttered, to the girl, to myself, and leaned the shotgun up against the wall. The blade of my knife caught the light as I took it down from its peg. "I have to."

The man looked up at me in pain and confusion as I seized a fistful of his hair and put my knife against his throat. The sheep crowded close, their nostrils flaring.

They knew what was coming.

I pressed the blade into his neck—but his girlfriend flung herself on me, grasping at the knife. Instead of a red flood, there was more of a spurt as my blade was pulled away, leaving only a small wound. The woman cried out as the sharp steel bit deep into her fingers instead, slicing them to the bone. Thunder pealed right overhead, rattling the old iron shed all the way to its foundations.

The sheep went mad.

I let go of the knife and stumbled back, jostled off my feet by their animal bodies. The blade hit the floor with a clang. *She* was there, in the thick of it, withered arms raised in triumph. As she looked over the couple, she pulled her thin, bloodless lips back in a feral smile. The blonde, crouching on the ground beside her partner, screamed as she saw *her*.

Then the sheep descended.

I had felt horror each time they rushed in to drink the blood hot from the trough, but this . . . I scrambled backwards until my shoulders hit the wall, and there stayed, cowering. My hands were shaking too much to even attempt to cover my face. The maddened ruminants shared *her* glow in their eyes. *She* threw back her head and cackled. The sheep's sharp hooves stomped, their blunt teeth bit. Their yellowed wool was stained dark red as they continued their frenzied attack. An overwhelming smell of copper filled the air as blood ran across the floor.

And the screams. Oh, the screams, amidst the bleating and baaing and the bitch's maddened laughing.

I turned to the side and vomited. Crawling on my belly, I found the strength to drag myself away from the nightmare, away from the harsh, bloodied light into the dark. Hot night air caressed my face. Protuberant clouds blotted out the stars above the farm, the first fat drops of greasy rain falling as I squirmed in the dust. My face was wet with it—or maybe that was with tears.

Writhing forward, my hand found the crumbled wood of the fence. I pulled myself to a kneeling position and looked up at the sign. Time and sun had wiped away many of the painted letters, but the last damning words remained.

"Welcome to Red's Farm. The Oldest Sheep Station in the Warrumbungle Shire."

About the Author:

Erin Munzenberger is a horror writer from Newcastle, NSW. She enjoys writing ghost stories and creature features, and has been published in both Australia and Canada.

Around 8,000 people go missing in Queensland each year. Most are found within 48 hours. But not all.

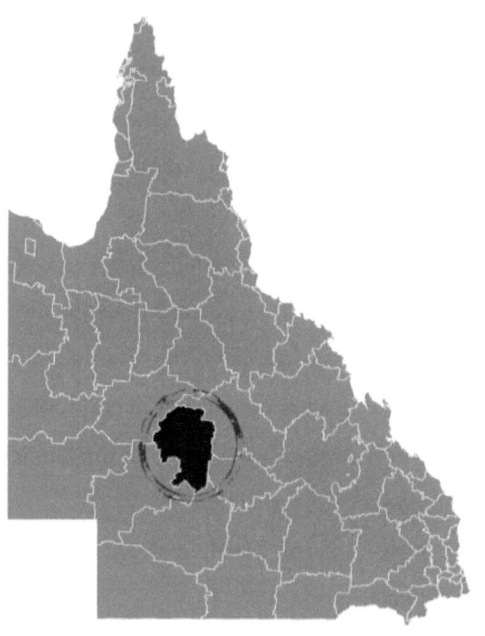

CLARRIE'S DAM

Rebecca Fraser

Old Clarrie shifted his bony frame in the worn wicker rocker and farted contentedly. He looked expectantly down at Rosie stretched beside him on the verandah. Without raising her nose from her paws, the Blue Heeler lifted an arthritic leg and parped her own flatulence into the afternoon heat. Clarrie laughed. It was their party trick.

Flo would have had plenty to say if she was here, but she wasn't. She'd taken the truck and headed east for the big smoke to see Katie's new sprog. He'd be five weeks old now, and Flo'd been fair champing at the bit to be there for the birth. But it hadn't been possible, what with the Big Wet and all. Even after the rain stopped they'd had to wait for the brown, churlish flood waters to recede. Burrawang Crossing was impossible to pass until three days ago. The Burrawang's banks–normally parched, ten-foot-high escarpments–had crumbled and collapsed into the foaming vortex that gnawed at her sides.

And so Flo had bided her time, knitting tiny articles of blue clothing, and squinting up at the sky with one ear melded to Clarrie's old radio. They'd come to rely on the battered old wireless quite a bit during the Big Wet, and Flo hung on every flood report for news of Burrawang. As soon as the announcer gave the green light that the Creek could be crossed with a suitable vehicle, Flo put down her needles and picked up her little square suitcase, which had been packed for days. She kissed Clarrie dutifully on the forehead and marched to the truck. Clarrie had smiled as the truck bounced down the long, jacaranda-lined driveway. She was a fine woman, his Flo, strong and resolute, a loyal worker and companion. Just like Rosie, really.

Plink. Plink. A pair of Pacific Blacks settled on the dam, their shiny beaks dipping in and out of the water. Clarrie smiled. The ducks were back. He hadn't seen them since the rain started. The first week after the drought broke, Flo had joked about gathering the pair up for the Ark they would surely need to build, but they never came. Nor did any other birdlife. The rain kept them confined to whatever secret spot birds inhabit when it is too wet to come out . . . even for ducks.

Rosie saw them too. Her tail thumped once, twice, on the wooden decking of the verandah, and her eyes formed lazy slits as she watched them skate back and forth. Clarrie had dug the dam for Flo; it would have been . . . what, forty, forty-two years ago now? She'd argued that every self-respecting farmer's wife should be able to enjoy the bounty of nature that a dam brings to the parched grasslands of remote Queensland.

They had other dams on their property, of course. Seven over ninety thousand acres, but they were working dams. Flo had wanted an ornamental dam close to the house that she could see from the shade of the verandah while patching Clarrie's jeans or oiling their saddles. So Clarrie had obliged and they'd enjoyed many a glass of iced tea, sitting together in comfortable silence on the verandah in the January twilight as the green-grey thunderheads rolled in from the south and electricity charged the air. The dam was at its most animated then, an oasis catering to a party of thousands. Crickets and cockatoos, cane toads and currawongs, bearded dragons and bandicoots, pythons and possums, all gathered at the fringes of the dam to drink their fill or snap at the midges and mosquitoes that teemed in fuzzy clouds over the surface.

Clarrie watched the ducks preen their feathers as they circled the new perimeters of the dam. There was a time during the Big Wet he'd feared the dam would be the undoing of their sanctuary, but while the water rose with an unnerving speed that crept towards the farmhouse, edging closer day by day until the bottom three verandah stairs were submerged, they had remained safe and dry. Even so, ten days after the heavens closed, the dam was still swollen to twice its size.

Plink. Plink. One of the Pacific Blacks sped across the dam, feet pedalling beneath the surface.

The other disappeared beneath the muddied water. It honked in fright and beat its wings as it was pulled downwards by an unseen force. The water where it had bobbed a second before threshed and churned.

123

"Struth," muttered Clarrie. He wrestled with the rocker in his haste to get to his feet. Rosie was already up and alert, tail down and ears forward. She growled softly.

"Easy, Rosie," Clarrie said. He gripped the smooth timber railing of the verandah and peered down at the dam. The remaining duck had taken flight and wheeled overhead in an anxious search for its mate. The dam was now peaceful and innocent, its surface as smooth as glass.

Rosie whined and looked up at Clarrie. He put a hand on her head and massaged one of her ears. His eyes darted this way and that, searching for a sign of the duck. For a full minute he scanned the brown water but there was not a ripple to be seen.

A jet of water burst forth from the dam. It spiked two metres into the air carrying a limp, black cargo. What was left of the duck was thrust up and outward from the bowels of the dam like a discarded rag. The misshapen carcass floated eerily on the surface.

Clarrie scrambled down the stairs, Rosie at his heels. He stopped at the edge of the dam and leant forward as far as he could. The body was out of his reach. Rosie put a paw into the water, her body braced ready to spring.

"No, Rosie! Sit. Stay." Clarrie barked his commands. Rosie looked up at him. "Sorry, old girl, but you can't retrieve this one. Dunno what's lurking in that water."

He poked about the fringes of the dam in search of an instrument to hook the battered duck to shore. The flood waters

124

had washed a detritus of objects across his property, and he selected a length of forked branch tangled in the fence line. That should do the job.

He returned to the edge of the dam and reached out with the stick. After a couple of tries, the forked branch snared around what was left of the duck, and he eased it back to shore. Rosie danced at his side with excitement, her toenails sinking deep into the squelching mud.

Clarrie inspected the duck, prodding it gingerly with his calloused fingers. The duck's head was missing. Both its legs were gone and only one wing was left, held to its shredded body by a strand of stretched, raw sinew.

"Jesus," Clarrie muttered. He turned it over in his hands. He knew the method of every predator in a thousand kilometre radius. This wasn't the work of any he'd seen. Too clean for a dingo. Besides, what would a dingo be doing in his dam? A bird of prey? No, not with these wounds. Even the talons of the mighty wedge tail didn't sever like this. In any case, he hadn't seen an eagle of any kind since the Big Wet.

"Gotta be an eel, Rosie," he said. "Can't be anything else. Yep, a bloody great eel, that's all I reckon it could be." He put down the duck and wiped his hands on the seat of his pants. Rosie leant forward for a tentative sniff. She growled and put her tail between her legs.

* * *

Clarrie judged it was somewhere close to two o'clock by the way the moon cast its shadow over the bedroom wall. He'd been asleep for four hours before the unknown thing woke him. It was the same every night, Clarrie reflected: long periods of wakefulness in the hours of night when his slumber should be at its deepest. Part and parcel of being an old bugger, he supposed.

He kicked off the thin sheet and lay on his bed in his yellowed cotton drawers listening to the night song of the cicadas. Flo's side of the bed seemed to stretch out for miles. He missed her. She would be back the day after next. He hoped she was having a good time with Katie.

Katie, who was always trying to get them to move to Brisbane, or Bris Vegas, or whatever it was called these days. He'd been there a few times of course, and hated every second. No, the Outback was for him and Flo. "You come and bury us on the farm, Katie, my love," he'd said on his last visit. "Your mother and I have already picked out our plots." He recalled laughing as Katie shook her head in exasperation.

The Big Wet had been a challenge, though. Week after week of sheet rain, the likes of which Clarrie had never seen. It broke dams, burst river banks, corroded roads and flooded plains that hadn't seen more than millimetres, probably since the Cretaceous Period.

At first Clarrie and Flo rejoiced. Cockies from neighbouring farms millions of acres away joined in prayers of thanks, their leathered faces lifted skyward to let the rain cleanse away the red dirt of seventeen years of toil and drought. But then it didn't stop and—

A terrible pain-filled scream sounded outside his bedroom window. The hair on the back of Clarrie's neck rose in protest. The scream abruptly cut off. What followed was a series of feeble whines that gave way to a dreadful drumming sound. *Rosie.*

Clarrie leapt from his bed and raced from the room. He threw open the front screen door. It banged against the side of the house. At first he couldn't make out waped and gaped. Rosie jerked and twitched under a writhing, oily shroud.

Clarrie kept his eyes locked on the shuddering mound while he groped for the old torch he kept on a hook by the front door. He snapped it on and directed the weak beam at Rosie. The torchlight presented a scene of such alien horror that Clarrie felt his bladder give way.

Rosie was under attack. Scores of—what the hell were they, fish? eels? salamanders?—worried at her throat, her head, her legs, her tail. Her belly, round with age, was split from breast to groin like some obscene autopsy. Countless tails thrashed and pulsed to push prehistoric-looking heads deeper into the bloodied fissure and pull at her entrails.

Clarrie sprang into action. He rushed forward swinging wildly with the torch, wielding it like a bludgeon by the hank of rope attached to its handle. The creatures dissipated in one menacing body and disappeared in a stream of inky-hided reptilia down the verandah stairs, towards the dam.

Rosie was still. He moved towards her. In the muted torchlight something dark and sinuous disengaged itself from her right ear and glided past him. Without thinking he brought his bare foot down. A satisfying squelch was followed by a burst of pain as the thing twisted underfoot and buried what felt like red hot knives into the tissue between his ankle and his heel. Clarrie screamed and shook his foot. The creature was flung against the side of the house and Clarrie beat at it with the torch until it stopped moving.

He turned back to Rosie. She was unrecognisable. So frenzied was the attack that only a few patches of fur remained. The rest of her body had been completely skinned, exposing flesh that in places was gnawed through to the bone. Her tail was reduced to a bloodied stump and her eyes, so alert and intelligent, were gone.

He keened and wept as he wrapped what was left of Rosie in the horse blanket. He carried her into the house and laid her gently on the kitchen table. Unsure of what to do next, he simply stood there. He was only aware of how much time had elapsed over his vigil when the first kookaburra heralded the break of the new day with its raucous laughter.

The encroaching daylight lent surrealism to the events of the previous night, and Clarrie shook off the cloak of shock that had bound him to the kitchen for the past few hours. His grief was no less, however, and the knife that turned in the pit of his stomach when he looked again at the misshapen mound of blanket on his kitchen table was cold and sharp.

He put a saucepan of water on the hob for coffee. There is a time to mourn and a time to act, his father used to say, and Clarrie knew it was the truth. If Clarence Snr was alive, he would have clipped Clarrie a good one around the ears and told him to firm up.

While he waited for the water to boil, Clarrie opened the front door and stepped cautiously onto the verandah. There was nothing to indicate that anything peculiar had taken place. The morning was bright and clear, and dawn's chorus of native birdsong echoed from the treetops. The dam was as serene as a mill pond.

Clarrie returned to the spot where Rosie had slept. Sure enough, there it was. The creature that bit him was still lying on the verandah. Clarrie made to poke it with his toe and then thought better of it. The wound to his foot still throbbed and wept tiny rivulets of blood when he walked. Instead, he bent down low with his hands on his knees and examined it from every possible angle.

When he was a boy, his grandfather had given him an encyclopedia for his eighth birthday. Clarrie had spent hours curled up under a shade tree between chores, transfixed by the wonders the book contained. One chapter was devoted to deep sea marine life, or, as the encyclopedia called them, "*Monsters of the Depths*". One particular photograph had fuelled Clarrie's imagination. It was a viperfish.

The creature on his verandah bore a strong resemblance to that photograph, from its long needle-like teeth to its distended mouth equipped with hinged jaw. It had the same elongated dorsal fin and blue-black eel-like body. Even the malevolent eye that stared up at Clarrie, causing him to shudder involuntarily, had the same distinction.

But that would be impossible. Viperfish lived in the ocean. Furthermore, they dwelled at depths of up to a kilometre and a half below the surface. Fish do not leave the water to walk on land. It simply could not be. Yet here it was. The memory of countless multi-fanged fish surging as one along the verandah when he'd startled them with the torchlight returned, and he shook his head in frightened wonder.

Clarrie located one of his old shoes and slid it under the fearsome-looking being. He realised it was long dead now, but he still couldn't bring himself to touch it. He raised it to eye level. There *was* something different about it that the viperfish in his book didn't have. Four tiny nubs sprouted from the flanks of its body. Each nub was fringed with a small suction cup, not unlike a gecko's foot. *Feet?* The bloody fish had feet!

Clarrie put it down and returned to the kitchen to prepare his coffee. He needed to think, but the stirrings of panic clamouring in his mind made it difficult. He'd heard of the evolutionary process where ancient species in times of drought had used their fleshy fins to heave themselves to land in search of water. Had the

Big Wet been the catalyst to something so unspeakable in his dam?

The coffee was hot and strong and Clarrie left out his usual milk. He did stir in three heaped spoonfuls of sugar as an afterthought. He forced himself to eat a hunk of Flo's homemade bread and chewed on it while he pondered what to do. Flo wouldn't be back with the truck until tomorrow. How far would he get by foot? Silly old fool, he remonstrated, it would be suicide to walk out onto the main road without a plan. Sometimes they didn't see another vehicle for months. The phone line had been out since week three of the rain, and there was no indication the phone company would be attending to its repair anytime soon.

One productive thing Clarrie could do was bury Rosie. When the sun moved across the sky and the intense heat of the middle of the day had dwindled to the calmer afternoon warmth, he dressed and pulled on his work boots. He gathered up his dog from the kitchen table, wincing at the wetness seeping through the blanket. He would take her out to the plots he and Flo had selected for their own passing and bury her next to them. Outside, he took a long look at the dam. The dead fish lay like an abomination on the verandah, and he kicked it as hard as he could. It flip-flopped down the stairs and Clarrie could feel its dead eye on him as he hoisted Rosie up and over his shoulder and carried her to the north side of the farm house.

There beneath the lilly pillies, he dug a grave for her. The ground was still wet and easy to turn. He wept again as the first sod fell on her blanketed side, and when the job was done he sat next to the fresh mound of copper earth and thought about the day he had brought Rosie home. He'd had his eye on her from birth, when the Joneses' bitch had whelped all those years ago, and she hadn't let him down. There had been others before her of course, but she had been special.

Clarrie suddenly felt very old. He would wait until tomorrow when Flo came back with the truck. Then they could leave together and drive out to the pub at Burrawang Crossing. They could ring the police, or CSIRO, or whoever it was you reported something like this to. For now, all Clarrie wanted to do was take a long bath, lock the doors against the horrors of the dam, and wait for Flo.

* * *

Clarrie closed his eyes and let the hot water work its magic on his bones. The bite on his ankle had smarted something terrible when he'd soaped it up, and he reminded himself to cover it when he got out. He rested one cheek against the cool porcelain of the tub and let his mind drift to a happier time. Katie in a blue smock dress, pigtails streaming out behind her as he pushed her on the tyre swing under the ghost gum. "Higher, Daddy, higher," she shrieked. The joy in her voice, the freckles on her nose—

Plink. Plink.

Clarrie's eyes flew open. Too late. Viperfish swarmed over the edge of the bath. They filled it in seconds, their ugly heads snapping and biting at whatever flesh they could find. The soapy water foamed red.

* * *

Flo hummed as she thought of little Samuel. Goodness, but he was a bonny wee chap. She couldn't wait to tell Clarrie all about him. Katie had given her some photographs to take back as well. Clarrie would be tickled pink by them.

She steered the truck deftly around a large pothole. The drive to Brisbane had been laborious with the new landscape carved by the Big Wet—and that had been in daylight. Now, cloaked by the deep blackness of the far western Queensland night, she slowed the truck to a crawl as she picked her way between furrows and craters in the uneven surface of the road.

At last she came to the familiar shape of the lone boab tree that marked the entrance to their driveway. She turned in, already thinking about the pot roast she would prepare for Clarrie's dinner tomorrow.

The truck's headlights picked up strange shadows on the road. Something fluid was moving along the driveway toward her. What could it be? More flood water? Surely not. And where was Rosie? Normally the old girl went mad with delight whenever a vehicle came down the driveway, a one-dog welcoming party, racing alongside and barking all the way to the farm house.

133

Flo suddenly felt uneasy. The lights were off in the farm house, too, but Clarrie was expecting her. He wouldn't have gone to bed, would he? If so, he would have left a light on for her.

She bumped the headlights up to high beam. The ground from the farmhouse to the truck seethed and roiled. She let out a scream and her hands flew to her throat. Gnashing teeth and threshing tails as far as the eye could see. Flo wrenched the gear stick into reverse, but it was too late. Even as she pumped her foot on the accelerator in blind panic, the truck let out a sighing hiss as a thousand razor-sharp teeth penetrated the tyre rubber.

The legion of viperfish surged up and over the bonnet of the truck and hurled themselves at the windscreen. Flo kissed the crucifix that hung on delicate silver around her neck. She wouldn't have to wait long.

About the Author:

Rebecca Fraser is an award-winning author of genre-mashing fiction for children and adults living on Bunurong / Boon Wurrung Land. Her work has won, been shortlisted for, and honourably mentioned for numerous awards including the Aurealis, Australian Shadows, Ditmars, and Mornington Peninsula Shire Mayor's Writing Award. Rebecca's publications include three middle grade novels, a collection of short fiction, and over sixty short stories, poems, and articles in various anthologies, journals, and magazines.

Rebecca holds a MA in Creative Writing. To provide her muse with life's essentials she copywrites and edits in a freelance capacity and operates StoryCraft Creative Writing Workshops…however her true passion is storytelling.

Say G'day at www.rebeccafraser.com

Facebook: @writingandmoonlighting

Twitter/Insta: @becksmuse

Cairns is a picturesque city between the Great Barrier Reef and the Great Dividing Range, and it's on a lot of people's bucket list for a reason. It might just be the last place they visit.

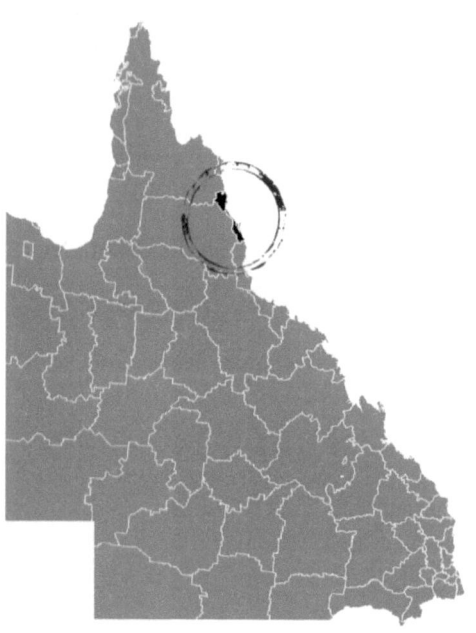

MIRI

Tim Borella

Little by little the sea was warming, too slowly for creatures living in and around the great coral reefs of northern Australia to register the existential threat, too fast for evolution's adaptive powers to respond. The one species equipped to comprehend the danger and perhaps counter it was, it seemed, incapable of united action, so even as tour boats and trawlers continued to criss-cross the opalescent waters as if all was well, once-thriving reefs bleached and died.

Alone or in great groups, heat-stressed coral reefs that had existed since the last ice age expelled zooxanthellae, their algal partners, consigning themselves to starvation. Complex food chains collapsed; what had been rich, colourful, bustling habitats for all manner and size of marine life turned with frightening speed into ghostly grey-white graveyards, devoid of nutrients.

But reefs in some form have graced the Earth for five hundred million years, and nature does not give up without a fight. When one way is blocked, she will find another.

* * *

I got to know Keith Elvey while I was working at a coffee shop near the Cairns marina, close to the finger where he moored his boat. He wasn't a customer, but I'd pass his berth most days on the way to drop off flat whites to Jean and David, a deeply tanned and wrinkled older couple whose live-aboard vessel, as far as I could tell, never left the dock.

Keith's boat, in contrast, was often out, but other times he'd be on deck cleaning, coiling up ropes and whatnot, and after a while we progressed from nodding terms to casual conversation, though I couldn't hang around long for fear of upsetting my boss.

"How's Benny the barista going?" he'd say in that laconic far north Queensland drawl.

"Steady steady thanks mate," I'd reply, trying for the tone the locals used.

The thing that really broke the ice was when I saw him splicing a rope, bringing the loosened strands of one end around to weave back in on itself and make a loop like a snake eating its own tail. Intent on his work, Keith didn't notice me until he'd tucked in the last strand and pulled it tight, testing the strength of his handiwork and nodding in satisfaction.

He looked up, saw me and winked. "That'll do the job, eh?"

"That's amazing," I said.

"Nah, just gotta know the tricks. I can show you, if you want."

I'd grown up in the 'burbs of Brisbane and had never been around anyone who knew how to *do* things. We didn't make stuff, we bought it.

"That'd be great," I said.

* * *

Instead of going straight home, I took to spending an hour or two after work with Keith on his boat, if he wasn't at sea. Home was a back room in a battered old Queenslander with a rusty corrugated iron roof, and though there were a few workmates I'd go out to a pub with now and then, I was floating along without much of a plan.

This new routine of companionable time spent in the wide estuary among the gently rocking boats filled some void for me. I'd be disappointed if I came to work and Keith's boat, *Miri*, wasn't there. I'd bring takeaway coffees and we'd sit and talk, but it was rare our time was spent idly. Keith always had something to do, and a knack of teaching things without me even realising it, like how to tie a reef knot or a bowline, or check the filters on the air compressor he used to fill up dive tanks.

Keith sometimes ran fishing and dive charters, but it didn't happen enough for him make a living out of it, and as we got to know one another better I realised he wasn't working as most of us think of it. Rather, he was living, using his boat to make a dollar or two when he needed to pay some bills, but just as often heading out to some remote reef to follow his passion for diving and exploring. He could easily feed himself spearing crays or pulling in a few coral trout, or turn them into money or barter goods if he wanted. It sounded like a dream to me.

It'd been an active wet season, but by April the weather began to cool down. Keith talked about how the steady south-easterlies would set in as the monsoon winds broke down and the sea surface temperature got too cool for cyclones, but as the great cycle changed, there would be a week or two of perfect weather for being out on the water. I was both excited and nervous when he asked if I'd like to come for a dive. I'd snorkelled a few times and was a fair swimmer, but wasn't confident about how I'd go with scuba gear.

"Don't you have to have a license or something?" I asked.

"Well, yeah," he said. "Don't stress though, Benny. Totally up to you, mate, but I've been teaching people for thirty years. Call it lesson one of your dive course."

My twinge of apprehension at the thought of serious water activities wasn't entirely unfounded. Tourists got into trouble just snorkelling around the local reefs and islands, and box jellyfish stings were being outstripped by sometimes fatal encounters with tiny irukandji, which you had no hope of seeing before they were on you. Crocodiles were turning up on popular beaches, and a spearfisher had recently been taken by a bull shark not far down the coast.

Keith was quick to reassure me when I brought it up. "Not speakin' ill of the dead, but as I heard it, he had fish in his wetsuit while he went after more. Not a great idea, Ben."

I nodded. "What do you reckon happened to that French couple, then?" The mysterious disappearance of two world travellers diving from their ocean-going sailboat at the outer reef had been all over the news the previous year.

"I'm not real sure about that one, to tell you the truth. The search was thorough, so unless they didn't want to be found they should've been. Hard to know, though. Maybe they got stuck in a crevice, or got too deep off the drop-off and just kept going down. The thing you've gotta remember is that it's the ocean. It's not our natural habitat, it's like walking into a jungle. I'd rather go doin' something I like than be hit by a bus crossing the road."

* * *

Miri had two big outboards, and once we were clear of the channel markers Keith opened her right up, standing tall at the wheel with his bronze-shot hair flying as the bow rose in response. Patches of light chop ruffled the otherwise glassy sea, and as we skipped along in the early dawn it felt like my senses weren't enough to take it all in, the rhythmic bump and sway of our movement, the salty tang and cool splash of spray on my lips and skin, the sublime wash of colour from eggshell blue above sweeping down to the hazy pink and grey mirage of the distant horizon.

The rugged green mass of Cape Grafton unfurled on our right, and our churning wake was a pointer back to the city nestled in its cradle between water's edge and coastal ranges, the silver white hotels dwindling as we ran eastward into the sunrise.

Skirting the low sandy oasis of Green Island, Keith leaned down, pulled a wetsuit from a big plastic crate and threw it to me. "Try that on for size, Benny."

He was already dressed in a knee-length suit, unzipped to the waist. I'd worn budgie smugglers under my T-shirt and boardies, and cringed at the contrast between my skinny whiteness and his tanned muscular frame as I struggled into the rubbery garment.

We must have driven for two hours before Keith pulled back the throttles and the bow sank back down. Low lines of breakers flagged the presence of large objects nearby, and as we crept forward, dark masses loomed below. The water was a beautiful clear cerulean blue now we were away from the churned sediment of the shallow coastal zone. There was an odd tang in the air, something between rotten vegetables and birdshit.

"Nearly low tide now," said Keith. "That smell's the coral slime. It makes its own sunscreen, did you know? Pretty amazing stuff."

We were right in amongst low dark fences of coral by now, some just breaking the surface, some still submerged, and I felt a twinge of unease. How weren't we hitting something? But Keith was as calm as ever, sure of his course.

"Run up the front, please mate," he said. "See the anchor?"

A hefty four-pronged hook attached to a chain rested in a metal tube at the front of the boat, with a neat coil of rope alongside.

"When I yell, chuck 'er overboard," Keith called. "Watch your feet don't get caught in the rope."

I did as I was told, the rope paying out a long way before Keith cut the motors and ran up to tie it off. The boat rocked and steadied as the anchor caught and held, and with the engine noise gone, the sounds of the reef enveloped us—waves breaking, a soft breeze, a flurry of baitfish jumping, seabirds calling to one another as they circled above or rested on the waves. It was utterly calming and magical.

True to his word, Keith took me through an basic dive course in record time, showing me how to clear my mask underwater, get my buoyancy right, sweep my arm round to find my backup regulator if for some strange reason the primary one failed.

"There's a lot to know, and you'll learn it," he said, fixing me with a stern look. "For today though, I only want you to remember one thing. If you have to come up fast, blow bubbles. Don't hold your breath—if you do, you're gunna burst your lungs, and we don't want that, do we?"

"No, we do not!" I said, apprehensive again.

He smiled. "Apart from that, just follow me and don't touch anything unless I do first. All good?"

Underwater was even more magical as we levitated among the clumps and plates, tendrils and towers of the coral structures. Though much of the reef had been hit hard by bleaching, this place had been spared. Keith led me from bommie to bommie, each a densely inhabited, fascinating sculpture drawing the eye ever deeper through levels of scale and intricacy, as compelling as any gallery exhibit.

Tiny creatures crawled and darted, stalked and hid while we hung godlike, observing. Then Keith pointed as a sleek grey reef shark cruised past, uninterested in us but reminding me of my true position in the food chain here.

Back on board, drying out in the warm sun, I knew I'd found something real. I wanted to grab hold of this new world, learn all there was to learn about it. We'd only been in the water for about an hour but I was yawning my head off, whereas Keith looked fresh as a daisy as he changed tanks on his rig. Still, I would have happily gone in again, but he had other plans.

"Sorry, Ben. I'm going pretty deep this time, and you need a bit more training before you can come along." He rummaged around on a shelf in the centre console and handed me a well-worn book. "Here, a bit of light reading for you."

It was a scuba training manual, something that by rights I should've already studied before getting to this point. I couldn't have been more motivated, though, and was actually looking forward to reading a textbook.

"I'll be back by midday," said Keith, and with that he was in the water and gone. I watched his trail of bubbles until I could no longer pick it out, and then it was just me and the sea. The wonder of my surrounds was a calming embrace, and I leaned on the rail and just took it all in as the swell gently rocked me.

A little later, nosing around the boat before sitting down to read, my attention was drawn to a large chart protected by a perspex panel showing the fish of the Great Barrier Reef in their myriad varieties. I recognised some from the dive earlier. Tucked in behind the perspex, too, was a photograph—a much younger Keith, bearded and grinning. A little girl clung to him like a koala on a gum tree, her smile matching his.

Curious, I slid a finger behind the panel and fished the photo out. Written on the back in pencil were the words '*Miri, age 7*'. Where was Miri now, I wondered. Or her mother? With a twinge of guilt, I returned the picture to its place.

On the run back in to Cairns, I asked Keith what he'd seen on his solo dive.

"Just something I've been keeping an eye on for a while," he said. "You always see something new, but there's been some changes going on with the deeper corals. I can't quite work out what's happening, but it feels—I dunno—important."

* * *

I'd gotten hooked on diving that first day, and stayed hooked. Keith was a natural teacher, generous with his time and knowledge. I was getting the good end of the deal (not that we ever spoke about deals) and took every opportunity to pay him back in kind, helping out as a deckhand on charters once I knew enough to be useful.

Tourist numbers were down so I was pulling fewer shifts at work, which freed me up to be out on the water more. That suited me fine, and what I learned in those months around the northern reefs was way beyond any cookie-cutter training course I could have done. I easily passed my online theory exam and got my ticket. Even better, Keith was now taking me on deeper and deeper dives.

* * *

As Keith put it, you didn't fuck around with deep diving. You had to adhere strictly to time and depth limits, or you'd be asking for the bends.

The reef we were diving on this time had been hard-hit. It was a vast depressing expanse of rubble, sand and sparse sea grass on the edge of the continental shelf, bounded on the seaward side by a protective wall of coral thousands of years old. Going beyond the wall was like falling off a cliff, and a rush of vertigo hit me as I looked down into the dark depths. Sunlight didn't penetrate far into the water, so we carried torches.

We descended, and our torches revealed unusual coral formations clinging to the wall. These were what Keith had been chasing. They were basket- or net-like, reminding me of something a child might make from rolls of clay, ranging from about fist-size to as big as a beach ball. Peering down, the shadows of even bigger ones loomed in the darkness.

Keith gestured for me to come closer, pointing to one of the baskets. It was a coral structure, with solid-looking bars. Inside was a flash of yellow and white, and, moving my torch around, I made out the unmistakable shape of a butterfly fish. Was it sleeping? Many fish used reef structures for protection. But something was wrong. Looking closer, thread-like protrusions joined the basket's inner wall to the fish, as if they were fused together.

I waved my hand, sending a current of water through the basket. The fish, which I'd now concluded was dead, sprang into action, thrashing against the restraining threads. Startled, I backpedalled, exchanging a look with Keith.

We moved on to other baskets, finding most empty, but some with other hapless fish, and in one, a good-sized cray.

Soon it was time to surface, but we needed a decompression stop first. Hanging in the water a few metres below the sunlit surface, I had time to think about what I'd seen. How would a fish get caught in something like that? What were those threads doing? I hadn't been around the marine environment long enough to know a great deal, but I'd never heard of anything like this.

Back on board, Keith didn't have many more answers than I did. "I've seen them before on other reefs, but nothing like as many or as big as these, and none with fish in 'em," he said. "I'm not a hundred percent sure, but think about it—there's bugger-all food anymore. Corals are animals, and an animal's got to eat."

"You think they're feeding on the fish?" I said.

"I do."

"But I thought they used algae, photosynthesis and all that?"

"The shallow water ones do, but deepwater corals don't have sunlight or algae. They grab food right out of the water, little creatures."

"These ones, though—how could you catch something big like that?" I said. "Maybe it stuns them, like an anemone."

"Maybe. One thing's for sure, they weren't doing much while we were watching them. I reckon we've gotta come back at night."

* * *

Looking back, we should have told someone what we'd found. The thing was, Keith didn't think in terms of getting recognition for a discovery, or the protocols of scientific research. He was just a bloke with an insatiable curiosity who wanted to figure something out, and I was his disciple.

A week passed before we could get back out again. Instead of leaving at dawn we went in the afternoon, anchoring up around five. We prepared our gear and waited for it to get dark, munching on ham sandwiches I'd brought along. The evening was calm and cool, the sunset mesmerising.

"Doesn't get any better than this, does it mate?" Keith said.

Once the sun dropped below the horizon, we stirred ourselves. I hadn't done many night dives, and my previous calm gave way to nervous energy. We cracked the lightsticks we'd tied to our tank valves. They'd glow red for hours, so even if our torches failed, we'd still be able to find one another if we got separated.

We entered the water, got our buoyancy sorted, and I followed Keith's torchlight as he led the way. Soon we'd crossed the wall and were descending. The limited scope of my torch beam made me claustrophobic, and I knew sharks were more active at night. I reminded myself to use a methodical scan pattern, building up a wider picture in my mind rather than focussing solely on the small cone of light.

Soon we reached the flattened ball shapes of the baskets squashed against the sheer drop-off wall. They didn't look any different to how they had in daylight. I'm not sure what I'd expected, but I knew Keith would be disappointed.

We passed the group we'd found last time and pushed deeper, looking for the larger specimens we thought might be down there. There were plenty of smaller ones dotted around, and I approached one, attracted by a hint of movement. I shone my torch through the bars and peered inside.

I didn't mean to touch the thing, but the altered perspective in the dark made me clumsy. As soon as my hand grazed the basket, something shot out and wrapped around my wrist. I almost spat out my regulator before I regained control of myself, straining to pull my hand away and waving my torch in Keith's direction.

Whatever had hold of me was strong, and as I struggled, another band wrapped itself over the first. Under the torch beam, what looked like one of the basket's bars, but wet-looking and flexible, was winding itself up my arm.

With one hand holding the torch and the other trapped, I couldn't adjust my buoyancy and drifted upward, anchored by my twisted wrist. I smashed at the stuff with my torch, fighting hysteria, and would have given up if Keith hadn't joined in with his dive knife, stabbing and slashing away at the hardening bars from below as I floated upside-down, waiting to die.

The combination of Keith's attack and a final excruciating twist of my wrist set me free, and through tears of pain I tried to calm myself, knowing that panic would kill me as surely as anything external. I picked a spot on the wall in the torchlight and fixed my buoyancy, stopping my upward drift.

Looking down, I found the glow of Keith's lightstick and— staying well away from the wall and its inhabitants–swam towards him. His voice was clear in my mind—*Calm down Benny, check your gear and make a plan.* We'd collect our thoughts, control our breathing and make our way back up to the decompression stop. Closing in on the dim red light, I checked my air gauge, surprised to see I was just into reserve, considering I'd felt like I was sucking the tank dry a few minutes ago.

But where was Keith's torch? I shut mine off and saw, far below, the slow spin of a faint beam spiralling down. He must have dropped it in the fracas, but that was okay. We still had mine.

I turned my torch back on as we drew level, shielding it with my injured hand to spread the beam and keep it from shining in Keith's face. As usual, he was steady in the water, buoyancy perfect.

Except it wasn't that holding him in place. Icy dread took hold of me as I played the beam over him. Thick layered bars of coral encased his body from shoulders to ankles, the biggest basket yet that must have reached up from below while he was saving me.

Life-sucking tendrils like umbilical cords in reverse had already penetrated his wetsuit.

Knowing what it had taken to break the hold on me, it would be futile to attack this much bigger creature, but I had to try. I raised the torch in my good hand and closed in, but as the light illuminated Keith's face, he shook his head, then jerked it upwards. He was telling me to go.

He'd taught me well, and I knew the equation. Air, depth, decompression stops—if I didn't go now we would both die here. Still, I could not leave, but I saw determination outweighed his agony. He narrowed his gaze, fixed me with that stare and willed me to abandon him. Then his eyes closed and his face turned upward like a martyred saint.

* * *

The rising sun woke me on *Miri's* deck. Shooting pains in my arm brought the back the night's madness and I dimly remembered making it to the boat desperate to get help for Keith, knowing I could neither get back to Cairns by myself in the dark or summon someone out who could do anything useful. There was an emergency beacon and I knew how to work it, but the cold fact of the matter was that my friend was surely dead twice over-oxygen starvation and the other primal, cruel way we had discovered.

Once I got my wits about me enough to start the motors and free the anchor, I turned my back on the rising sun and drove until I found familiar landmarks. Not so much arriving at the dock as crashing into it, I tied the ropes off, grabbed my phone and dialled triple zero.

* * *

"You're certain this is the spot?" the sergeant asked again.

"Sorry," I said. "Yes, I'm pretty sure, but it was night time. I think so."

"He thinks so." He turned to the constables, eyebrows raised. They were already suited up. "Okay boys, as we discussed, a standard recce down the wall. Watch your gauges and each other, and I'll see you back here at zero nine thirty."

"Yes, sarge." The two men slipped into the water and disappeared below.

The sergeant marked the time on his clipboard, then turned for the stairway leading to the bridge, motioning for me to follow.

We sat in silence opposite one another at a small table. I'd told my story to several different officers and nobody showed signs of believing me. I couldn't blame them, and though I'd done nothing wrong, that wasn't the point.

Two of us had gone out on Keith's boat, and only one had come back. The possibilities—excluding staged disappearance, which wasn't unknown in these parts—were accidental death, or something more sinister. My statement sounded like a work of fiction, so until some corroborating evidence was found, here we were.

In the whirlwind of activity since my return, I hadn't had time to grieve for Keith, but now the weight of it settled on me. I lowered my head onto my crossed arms and cried as quietly as I could, and to his credit the sergeant reached over and laid a comforting hand on my shoulder.

I stayed there for a long time, numb, until the sergeant got up and went downstairs. Wiping my eyes, I took a deep breath and followed, surprised to see it was already a quarter to ten.

The divers hadn't returned.

We waited half an hour. The sergeant paced the deck, his nervous movements at odds with his mask of professional calm.

A cold certainty settled over me. He didn't know what I knew. "I don't think they're coming back," I said.

He opened his mouth as if to protest, but said nothing. I saw the mask slip.

Then he ran for the radio.

About the Author:

Tim Borella is an Australian author of speculative fiction. He contributes to AntipodeanSF, and has recently had stories published by Deadset Press, Horrorsmith Publishing, Third Flatiron Publishing, Nightmare Fuel Magazine and others. He's also a songwriter, and has been lucky enough to have spent most of his working life doing something else he loves, flying. Tim lives in Far North Queensland, on country recognised as the home of the Ngadjon-jii people. More information is available at tim-borella-author.mailchimpsites.com or on his Tim Borella - Author facebook page.

Mount Tambourine is a hidden paradise at the southern end of Queensland. You could spend a day exploring the rainforest, or the rest of the life.

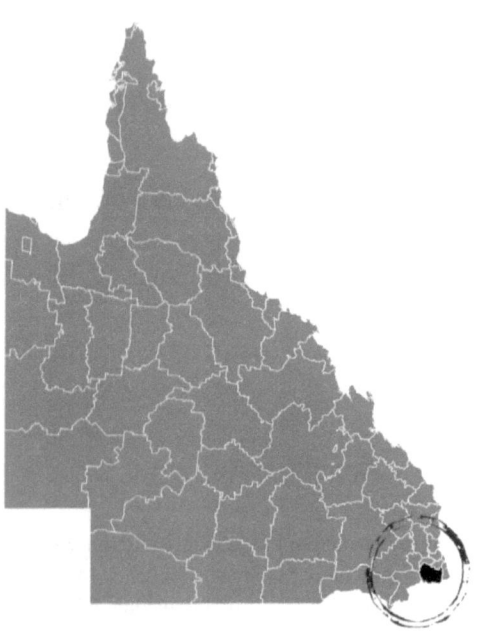

THE CURSE OF CURTIS FALLS

Jo Hart

Curtis Falls, Mt. Tamborine, November 1965

The sun blazed high in a clear cornflower-blue sky. The air rippled in a hazy way. Sweat prickled beneath Lotty's polyester dress. The pattern of palm leaves may have looked the part, but the dress had not been made with the muggy Queensland heat in mind. Nancy and Marge's cotton dresses were much more appropriate, but then they were used to living in Queensland, unlike Lotty.

"Come on, Lotty," Nancy called out. "You'll feel much better once we get to the rainforest."

Lotty put a hand to her hair to ensure her combs were still in place as she hurried to catch up to her two companions and lamented the effect the humidity had on her usually sleek French roll. "You might have warned me about the weather."

"We did," her friends chorused, each linking elbows with her, one on either side.

"But you didn't tell me how *sticky* it would be."

"Typical Victorian," Nancy said, rolling her eyes.

Lotty had been about to retort that they'd once been Victorians themselves, but gasped as the path took them beneath an arch of deep green and she found herself surrounded by rainforest.

Marge and Nancy swapped knowing looks and pulled at Lotty's elbows to keep her walking forward.

The temperature dropped to a comfortable coolness in the shade of the dark canopy. Dappled sunlight filtered through the treetops, but bore none of the muggy heat. The three walked for a while in reverent silence. Birds called to each other above their heads, insects hummed and a chorus of frogs warbled. Soon the gurgle of water rushing over rocks added to the rainforest song.

The magical majesty of the rainforest left Lotty in awe, from the moss-covered rocks to the twisted roots of trees whose names she did not know.

The path narrowed so that the three girls had to walk in single file. Beside them a creek splashed over smooth stones and glinted in the sunlight. They stopped on a narrow concrete bridge crossing the creek to delight in the eels and turtles swimming below, even catching sight of an elusive platypus. Marge and Nancy turned to continue, but Lotty remained mesmerised by the glittering world beneath her feet.

She did a double take. Could it be? Beneath the surface, Lotty could have sworn she saw a watery face appear, but as quickly as it had appeared it was gone again. Lotty knelt down on the bridge and searched the shallows, but found no sign of the face.

"Come on, Lotty!" called her friends, gesturing for her to catch up.

Lotty stood, dusting the dirt from her dress and giving her head a little shake. Perhaps even on the cool rainforest path she was being affected by the tropical heat. She said not a word to her friends about the face when she caught up to them again.

Less than an hour after setting out, the three friends arrived at the magnificent waterfalls. A wall of white spray fell like a curtain and splashed into a turquoise pool to feed the creek. The rocks at the foot of the falls were coated in a wet sheen. All around the falls lush greenery grew in abundance in the deepest hues of emerald and jade, adorning the cliff face like leafy jewels.

"It's like paradise!" Lotty exclaimed.

The three women left the path and teetered and balanced across the rocks, taking great care so they wouldn't slip on the wet and mossy surfaces. By the falls, the wildlife was even more abundant. Birds chorused about them—some even approached the water's edge on the opposite side of the pool. Dragonflies flitted over the blue-green surface, avoiding the hungry mouths of fish whose heads bobbed above the water to capture lunch.

Shucking off their shoes, the girls lazed on the rocks, giggling and chatting without a care. A fine mist from the waterfall kissed their skin.

Lotty had become mesmerised by a dragonfly with a shiny peacock-blue body when a shadow passed across the water. She looked over her shoulder, expecting the arrival of another walking group, though she'd not heard their approach. But Lotty and her two friends were the only people present in this little piece of heaven. She looked back into the blue shallows and almost fell into the pool in shock. This time she was sure she had seen a face, as transparent and rippled as the water itself. She could have sworn that it smiled at her before it floated into the roots of a palm.

Lotty's heart beat a little faster, for it had not been a pleasant smile. "Shall we get going?" she asked, trying not to let her fear show. The girls would think she was being silly, imagining faces in the water.

"Oh no! We can't go yet, we just got here," Marge exclaimed.

Nancy pulled some sandwiches and lemonade from her pack and shared them out, then leaned back with a copy of *Vogue* and flipped through the pages while she ate.

Lotty took a seat on a fallen branch a good distance from the water's edge. She couldn't shake the feeling of that face still watching her as she ate. A shiver ran up her back as she glanced at the pool.

"Isn't it a glorious day?" Marge sighed, tilting her face towards the sunlight filtering through the trees.

A hint of breeze brushed by, lifting errant leaves and causing ripples in the water. Lotty sipped on her lemonade. The sweet bubbles tickled her tongue. She tilted her face back, letting the dappled light dance across her cheeks, and soon her thoughts drifted away from the malevolent face in the water. The waterfall was so serene, the sunshine so warm, and the breeze so playful.

"I must get a photograph," she said, remembering her new Polaroid camera in her bag. "You two stand there with the falls behind you."

They shook the crumbs from their skirts and Lotty directed her two friends so that they were in frame. They stood with arms around each other's shoulders and smiled while Lotty focused the lens and clicked the button. "Perfect!"

The girls came beside her as they waited for the square of photo paper to come out. Lotty took the square and shook it. After a few moments, the image appeared—two girls standing before a green backdrop and a splashing waterfall.

Lotty frowned at the image. The way the shadows fell on the water behind them made it look like something lurked beneath the falls. Lotty discarded the thought from her mind. It was a shadow, that was all. There were no strange faces or figures in the water. It was far too shallow for a start, and neither Marge nor Nancy were aware of anything odd. They'd walked this trail many times, or so they had told her, so they would know if there was anything strange about this place. Wouldn't they?

Another gust of breeze brushed by. It took hold of the image and snatched it from Lotty's hand.

"Oh!" She tried to grab it back, but the wind carried it up above her friends' heads and over the pool, letting go right in the middle where they could not hope to reach it. It fluttered and twirled down towards the water, landing face up and floating like a lily pad.

"We'll just take another," suggested Nancy, but as she said it several spots of rain splodged against their arms and faces.

The sky had turned from cornflower blue to charcoal grey. The last rays of sunshine were being devoured by voluminous clouds.

"We didn't even bring umbrellas," said Marge. "We'll have to make a run for it."

"We'll be soaked by the time we get back to the car," said Nancy as she picked up her bag.

Lotty, however, welcomed the cool shower. Even in the shady rainforest the warmth had been stifling; she'd never sweated so much in her life! She looked about for her shoes and realised she'd left them by the water's edge. As she reached for them the Polaroid floated towards her. It came so close that Lotty thought she might be able to reach it.

"Are you coming?" Marge's voice pulled her attention from the water. "I'm getting drenched."

Both Nancy and Marge had slipped on their shoes and stood there waiting to leave. Nancy sheltered herself with her copy of *Vogue* and Marge held her bag above her head.

"Oh, yes, just one more minute," Lotty replied, returning her gaze to the rippling pool in hopes of catching hold of the photo.

Tentatively she reached out and caught the corner of the Polaroid between her fingers. The tip of her middle finger trailed into the cool water.

All of a sudden, the water turned jet black. It churned and bubbled. Before she could pull her hand away, something formed a tight grip around her wrist. Her mouth opened to scream, but she was pulled under before she could make a sound. Though the pool had looked shallow, it felt as though she plunged to a great depth. She thrashed and kicked. Lotty prayed her friends would see she was in trouble and rescue her. But they must not have been able to help, because the only hands that gripped her pulled her downwards.

Falling.

Sinking.

She fought against the need to draw in a breath. Her legs kicked furiously and her arms tried to claw their way back to the top, but to no avail. The invisible force pulled her forever downwards. As her lungs screamed at her, she pinched her lips together as tight as possible to keep herself from taking the breath she desperately needed. The uncontrollable gasp for breath came anyway and her lungs filled with water.

A watery figure swam circles around her. A translucent girl with hair like seaweed fanned out around her head and a sadistic grin twisting her blue-tinged lips. Her gurgled laughter filled Lotty's head, drowning her senses as the water drowned the life from her. *Who are you?* Lotty wanted to ask. *Why are you doing this to me?*

Lotty's limbs grew weak as she tried to fight. Her head filled with a dull fog. Blackness overcame her. The laughter faded and the only sensation she felt was the feeling of floating.

Floating.

* * *

Marge and Nancy reached the path and turned back to call to Lotty. Both froze, confused. Only seconds before their friend had stood by the water's edge, now there was no sign of her, save for her white shoes and satchel bag. Another girl whom they did not recognise stood by the pool, soaked from head to foot by the pelting rain. Her long skirt and puff-sleeved blouse were somewhat old-fashioned.

"Did you see where our friend went?" Nancy called to her.

The girl shook her head. She glanced at the falls, a guilty look flashing across her face. Then she took off down the path, laughing.

"I wonder why she's so happy," Nancy said.

Marge had no interest in the girl. Her concern was for her missing friend. "Lotty?" she called, looking about.

"Perhaps she needed to use the bushes," Nancy suggested.

"In the rain?"

Nancy shrugged. "Watch out for echidnas," she called out, laughing.

Five minutes passed and Lotty did not return. The girls' wet dresses clung to their bodies.

Marge bit her lip. "You don't think she got lost, do you?"

"Oh, what if she slipped and fell in the water!" Nancy started back towards the falls.

"We'd have heard a splash, don't you think?" Marge said, following all the same. "And it's far too shallow there."

They checked anyway, peering into the blue-green water as rain drops caused tiny ripples everywhere. Beneath the blurry surface they saw only fish and rocks.

Their calls echoed through the trees, but Lotty did not reply. Not knowing what else to do, they picked up Lotty's shoes and bag and hurried away to find a phone and call for a search party.

* * *

Men in bright yellow raincoats trudged through the forest under an ever-darkening sky, with torches and walkie-talkies, calling Lotty's name. The following day—with the sun bright once more and temperatures soaring into the nineties—the search continued. No sign of Lotty could be found, not a scrap of torn clothing nor trace of blood nor errant hair comb. It was as though she had disappeared from the face of the Earth.

"Any sign of her would have been washed away with the rain," a police officer told Marge and Nancy. "We'll keep searching, but the odds are against us."

In the years that followed, right up until their dying day, Marge and Nancy would never discover what happened to their friend.

Lotty's eyes flickered open. She had no idea how long she'd floated in the blackness. She knew by the stillness of the water that it had stopped raining. Glittery sunlight reached toward her, made wavy by the water in which she was immersed. Fish swam between her legs and over her stomach. Her hair fanned out around her like long tendrils of seaweed. What had happened to her combs? What had happened to her clothes, for that matter? She kicked experimentally. Her movement through the water caused no ripples or splashes. It felt as though she was a part of it, as though the water was an extension of her limbs. She came to rest near the edge of the pool so she could stare at the way the light and shadows moved like shapes in a kaleidoscope through the lens that was the water's surface.

The rippled face of a young girl appeared above her. The girl did not notice Lotty amongst the stones and fallen branches. At least, she didn't show any surprise to see a body floating beneath the surface. The girl's small hand reached toward the rippled divide. Lotty reached out her own hand. Their fingers were mere inches from each other. Lotty willed those small fingers to break the surface, but another hand grasped the child's and pulled her arm away. The woman's muffled words penetrated the water and reached Lotty's ears.

"You mustn't touch the water, child," the voice chided. "This pool is cursed. There be some bad spirits down there. They pull you in. They take your soul."

Lotty swam to the bottom of the falls, where the water bubbled and became opaque. The figure who had pulled her into the pool was gone now, of this she was sure. As she floated, turning over so at times she was upside down or on her back or on her side, her thoughts also floated and tumbled until she came to the only logical conclusion. When that girl had pulled her into the water, Lotty had taken her place. So all she needed to do to be free was pull another unsuspecting victim in and she could return to her life. Perhaps that was why she was so drawn to that little girl's hand as it reached towards her. Something inside her wanted to be free and knew by instinct how to escape this watery prison.

She flipped over again and swam towards the surface. The family had gone and Lotty could only see the rippled bodies of dragonflies flitting above.

One day someone would touch the water, and then she'd take them.

It was just a matter of time.

About the Author:

Jo Hart is a speculative fiction author from Gippsland, Victoria (Gunaikurnai country). Deadset Press published her Aurealis Award winning cli-fi novella *The Jindabyne Secret* as part of their Drowned Earth novella series. She loves writing speculative short fiction set in Australia and has a variety of short stories published in anthologies and online.

You can find out more about Jo's writing on her website: johartauthor.com
Follow her on social media for updates on her latest works:
facebook.com/JoHartAuthor - instagram.com/jo.hart.author

*The Kakadu National Park is the home to the
Saltwater Crocodile, the largest reptile in the world
and the most dangerous animal in Australia.
Don't forget to bring a towel.*

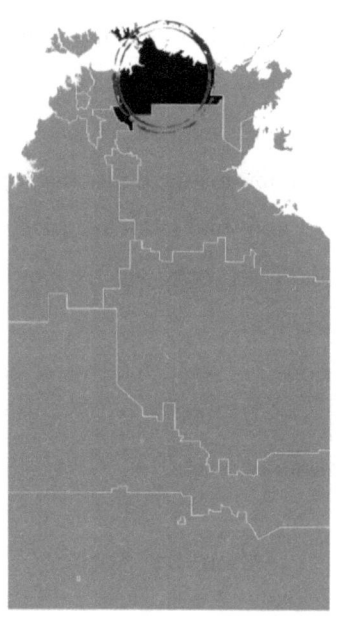

TERRISWALKERIS
TERRAEREGINAE

Eleanor Whitworth

We wake to find their bodies stretched ribbon-like around our little hidden camp. Long as our arms and blue as the sky, the worms move amongst the brown, curled leaves that have fallen with the overnight rain. Trailing through the muddy remains of our fire, they glint as bright as the rarest feather. They slide under us, unafraid of our weight, emerging unharmed from the other side of our bed-bark where we sit still and watching.

Bricaat had found one yesterday morning, her yelp turning me on my heel. "Look," she'd said, pointing at the bright, blind head that poked up out of the earth swaying slowly as if tasting the air.

Mesmerized, we'd let our precious pre-dawn time burn up with the rising sun, and went hungry as a result. As sweat slipped over our skin, we'd become fidgety and afraid of the worm's beautiful brightness, worried it would attract attention from something or someone, so we'd covered the creature carefully, laying leaves over it and standing a stick so we'd remember where not to step.

And this morning they are everywhere, too many to hide. We should be afraid, we should leave our camp, but there is something comforting about their rhythmic squeeze and stretch, plump and taut. I smile and nod at Bricaat. She gets up, stretches her arms. We cannot go another day without food. Picking up her pouch, she heads out into the bush, turning to wonder at the worms as she goes. Her skin is the colour of old-leaves and she soon disappears amongst the trees. This natural camouflage helps me relax a little.

I busy myself checking the contents of our run-bags. Our dried insects have fuzzed with mould. I wipe them off and pick out the four worst for us to eat today. I check the holes we have dug to try and trap a lizard or skink. But they are empty. They are always empty. I check the camp—careful to step around the ever-moving blue arcs—and shake the water off the sagging trees so they spring up to better hide our little home. The sun is now over the horizon and already the flurry of insects settles. Soon it will be too hot to move at all. Already tired I sit back against our stone overhang and wait.

My heart swells with love for this camp. From a distance it does not look like much. The overhang is hidden by bushes, but underneath is protection, and up close is beauty. The stone, made up of so many grains, reminds me of the irises of Bricaat's eyes—flecked and marked with a world of colours and textures and ridges that are as deep as forever. And across the stone are lines, clear and purposeful, that have been drawn by other hands long ago. The faint red marks are so faded we can't see the pictures they once were. But we don't mind, it is good to be in company, to know that this place has looked after others, and that others have looked after it.

* * *

The night we ran away from our village, we kept the pointer stars, those two bright eyes in the sky, behind us to watch our backs. This way, we knew we were running towards the poisoned land. We were afraid, not knowing what we would find when we got to the place they called *Jabiluka*. Would there be monsters, hungry from their life on ravaged lands? Would they reach out and grab us with the illness that had seized others? We had no choice, though. Running was our best chance of survival because our villagers would only follow us so far.

We went as fast as we could, but it was never fast enough. We stopped only once that first night, so thirsty we took a drink from a stream. As we caught our breaths, the pool of water settled so that we saw the half-moon swaying there. Side-by-side we looked down at our reflected faces. They were thin and sharp and surrounded by hair tufted like the afternoon clouds. Our eyes, identical in shape, not large not small, were so clear. Then something moved in the bush and we froze before running again until the sun rose and we found some bracken to lie in and hide from the heat and from our people.

It was Bricaat who found Jabiluka, raising her arm to stop me. "Listen," she'd said.

On one side of us the cicadas' trill was so loud it filled our heads and cleared our thoughts. On the other, everything looked the same: the plants growing with the same big fat leaves and the vines just as busy climbing. But it was dead quiet.

"This is it," Bricaat said. "We will follow this edge."

The next day, we came to an old sign, folded over like it was bowing to the earth, a tangle of spiked metal fence cascading out behind it. Bricaat crouched to look closer, and I did too. We could not understand the words: RANGER MINE. NO ENTRY. RADIOACTIVE SITE. But the skull that sat above them, looking back at us through the moss and rust, made the meaning clear.

* * *

Bricaat returns from her foraging and spread her little collection of berries and tubers. "You start," she says.

I nod and take a berry, squeezing it with my tongue, the tang of it spreading through my mouth.

Bricaat takes one for herself.

"I will make it today," I say. "You rest." I pull my grinding stone from my run-bag and start crushing the three finger-like tubers just as I'd watched the villagers do. When the paste is smooth, I add a pinch of the furry good-smelling leaves and mix them in to help the paste stay down in our stomachs. I pass it to Bricaat. The worms still move around us. Their brightness makes me happy, but just as fast a chill shakes my spine.

I remember the first time we ate a worm, its brown body becoming a thin pink as my fingers pulled it from the earth under our cage. It curled and twitched as I held it between my teeth and bit it in two. The half I passed to Bricaat dropped and I caught it, having to close my hand around it as the other half flicked in my mouth. Could these worms know about that?

We finish breakfast. The sun is up and the heat is already pushing us back and down against the cool of the rock. We watch the worms make their way under the leaf litter as the air thickens with moisture. Billowing clouds form, soon to open upon us. I check the drainage channels around our camp, clearing leaves as the first heavy drops hit the ground. We sit in the small, dry area and place crumbs from the paste to see if the worms would like some. We know it's unlikely, but it is nice to share.

* * *

Everyone in our village shared in the celebration feasts. They even gave us bits of lizard meat. At the end of these nights, when their bellies were full, their bitterness eased and sometimes they would even laugh. They would dare to glance at us and make plans for the biggest of all the celebrations—the day we were as tall as our mother's waist and could be offered to the god so that the losses of our ancestors would not be repeated. They would rehearse the night of our offering, retelling the journey that our ancestors were forced to make out of their city, Daa-win, as their homes were swallowed by the sea. How the leftover land sickened with salt, and the heat became even more extreme, turning the daytime into a glaring enemy. How so many animals died, and people too from hunger and hate. How they travelled inland toward the rising sun to where the country is high. How the huge storms tried to stop them, and how one almost succeeded when it ripped the children from the arms of their families and carried them off over a cliff. Those children taken to become children offered.

Our mother, when she did care for us, did so with accusing eyes, her grief festering, as if it was our fault that we were the first born after the last child was offered. Our father didn't need to look away from us because he didn't look at us at all, even as he steered our younger brother off in other directions away from our cage, even as the boy tilted his head to catch our eyes. They treated us like nothing, and that is what we almost became.

* * *

Twilight arrives as the clouds rumble their rain off elsewhere, their billowing towers lit golden by the setting sun. Lingering drips make their final falls and the worms move again. We stay sitting and watching under the care of our rock. The worms weave around us and we realise that they are making a pattern. As the sky darkens, the worms become light, as if they have absorbed the day and now share it back out to the night. And as they brighten, the shapes they make come alive.

* * *

We got so unwell in our cage. Our growth slowed. The villagers were anxious to get their celebration done and were forced to feed us better food. Because they could not bear to look at us, they did not notice that we were loosening the binding at the far end of the cage, that we were hoarding little pieces of food, that we were strong because we had each other.

But we did start growing again, and one morning they stood our mother next to our cage and pulled us out to stand beside her. Using their hands they measured us up, bumping us against her shaking legs as her tears dropped to the ground at our feet. As their hands travelled from the tops of our heads across to her waist, their faces filled with relief. Plans could be made: drying wood, gathering food. The night before our celebration was the night we pulled the cage open and slipped out. A part of us—even though we had never spoken of it—hoped that we might find the group of people the villages called the Others. Would they know more kindness?

On that second night that we ran through the bush—the night that we were supposed to be offered—there was no rain. We kept moving, both of us thinking of the villagers, of how far they might follow us, of how they would be looking at the sky, supposed to be so happy that there was no rain so the fire could be big. But the clear sky soon darkened with clouds. A restless wind picked at the leaves around us. It got stronger and was soon bending the trees. We stopped and sheltered beneath a large rock. The huge clouds did not drop water, but it was as if this withholding made them even

173

more angry. They churned and whirled and lightning found and split the ground. Thunder cracked around us. We bowed our heads and covered our ears. Were the villagers right: were we needed, had we angered the god? But Bricaat shook her head and reminded me of the great storm that had come one time to the village, tearing down the small shelters. It had come anyway, and so had this storm. This was nothing to do with us. None of this was our fault. Then a sick orange appeared from the direction of the village. The wind carried the smell of smoke and something else: the smell of burning flesh.

"It is gone," Bricaat said.

"Yes," I replied.

A deep sorrow came upon us. Because fear can still make for attachment.

* * *

I wonder why the worms have come to us. Do they see us, or smell us, or feel us? They are so bright in the no-moon sky. As they make their pattern, intricate and beautiful, they leave a trail, a colour so blue and so filled with sparkling light that it could have been given by the stars. As they move, the squeeze and pull of their bodies asks us if they can include us within it. We moved towards them and they crawl up onto us, drawing lines and circles up and down our legs and arms and bodies and hair. Some of them climb the walls behind us. They are tracing the lines we knew so well, but also the lines we could not see. Our cave comes alive with the drawings of animals long gone and spirits maybe gone or maybe still amongst us. We stand up and sway and allow ourselves—for the first time—to be bright, to be as big as ourselves.

We do not sleep at all during the night, we save it for the daytime when the worms return to where they came from. And when the next evening arrives, we will eat the remainder of the insects and prepare. We know now that it is time for us to leave this special place, that it is our turn to give back, to see if we can find other people and other ways. It is time for us to grow into the next version of ourselves.

About the Author:

Eleanor is an Australian author living in Sydney, on Gadigal lands. Her work has been published in a range of journals and anthologies including *Meanjin, Meniscus*, *SQ Magazine, Not One of Us,* Deadset Press, B-Cubed Press and Black Hare Press. She is also part of the ACT Writers Hardcopy alumni. Find out more about her various activities and writing adventures at eleanorwhitworth.com

Folk from other states say that if you visit Adelaide,
the biggest risk you face is having a bad time.
The locals know better.

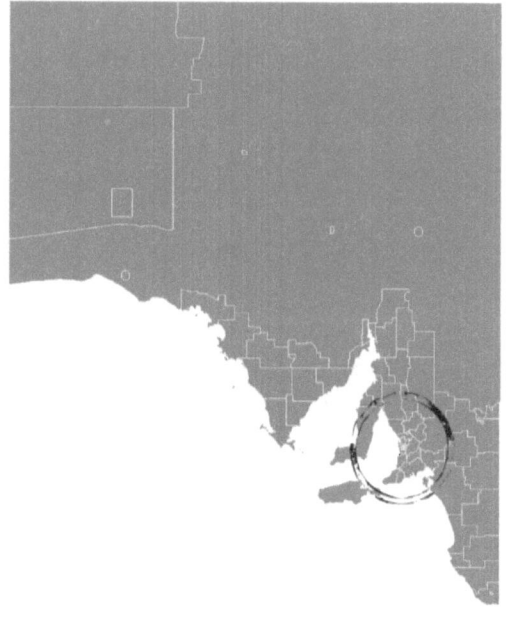

TRASH AND TREASURE

Matthew R. Davis

The car stereo's digital display ticked over to 12:00 as they pulled up at the kerb outside Mercury's Hoard Collectables, where the streetlights cast their hazy orange glow down to shine in puddles of rain like midnight suns. Colin twitched the ignition off, bringing The Cure's "Grinding Halt" to an appropriate conclusion as Jackie peered through her wet-spackled window at the bric-a-brac piled up on the footpath, already slipping off her seatbelt and reaching for the door with one eager hand.

"Midnight on a Friday night," Colin said, "and here we are, picking through junk on the street. Let no-one say we don't know how to party."

"Ain't no party like a street junk party," Jackie declared. "This is my jam! Half the stuff in my flat is preowned."

"Only half? You're the Op Shop Queen."

"Exactly. One man's trash is your lover girl's treasure." Jackie cracked the passenger door and sidestepped into cool night air.

Usually meticulous about her appearance, tonight she was dressed down: old acid-wash jeans with the knees frayed through, the long black velvet coat she'd scored cheap from a Salvation Army store, a faded *Adventure Time* T-shirt that she only wore when cleaning the flat, battered boots with spatters of yellow paint on the toes. Her jumbled outfit reflected the spontaneous nature of their expedition—just thirty minutes ago, she'd been sitting on her lounge in pyjamas, bare feet tucked beneath her as she perused Facebook. But then she'd given a purr of interest and leaned over to show Colin the latest post by Mercury's Hoard: a photo of their shopfront obscured by trestle tables piled high with intriguing miscellanea. *Freely given*, the post read, and *anything may be taken*.

Today had been the store's last day of business, and now they'd put out hundreds of unsold knick-knacks to be taken by anyone who cared to cruise by. Jackie's raised eyebrow had been a challenge, and Colin was game. They were having a lazy night in anyway, and besides, he loved to trawl through junk shops and collectables almost as much as she.

They'd visited Mercury's Hoard before, one sybaritic Saturday a few months back, lazy and glutted after a morning's repeated lovemaking; he'd found a few classic horror paperbacks, and she the set of bronze pebbled glasses that currently sat mouths-down on her kitchen sink. Jackie had recently mentioned the store was moving on and suggested a final visit, but only now were they making their appearance, as the clock ticked over from one day to the next and the street lay silent and still as an empty stage beneath the bittersweet tangerine glow of the sodium streetlights.

Many of the houses along this road were dark and lifeless, as well they might be at this time of night, but Colin couldn't help imagining for a moment that the street was one long shelf, the homes on it yet more discarded items left out for scavengers to rifle through. Black windows stared blindly back at him, deaf to the occasional car that hissed along the wet bitumen behind bright white eyes; traffic lights stood sentry at the T-junction a few metres along from Mercury's Hoard, currently beaming green as if encouraging him to get started on this late-night rummage.

He joined his girlfriend on the damp footpath outside the shopfront. They were alone here, and the junk-piled tables sheltering under the jutting roof had barely been touched. The weathered yellow strip sign over their heads declared the store's wares to be CLASSIC–UNIQUE–TIMELESS, and a fresher, handwritten one in the front window noted that the owners were STILL SNAPPING UP SELECTED TREASURES.

Jackie was already sifting through a bowl of pins and badges on the first table, and Colin stepped up alongside her to consider what the second had to offer. A set of antiquated stereo speakers with a power-cable tail that ended in a plug type he didn't recognise; a Tupperware container stuffed with ancient *Boys Own* annuals growing puffy and bloated like fungus in the wet; a rag-tag platoon of mismatched salt and pepper shakers; a collection of ugly fringed lampshades stacked atop each other like tacky witches hats; an old brass magazine rack stacked with wrinkled LP sleeves, nothing newer or more interesting than Kenny Rogers' *Greatest Hits*.

"Aha!" Jackie triumphantly brandished a *Yellow Submarine* badge before tucking it into the pocket of her velvet coat. "Sweet! This could be a long night, honey—there's so much stuff here."

She wasn't wrong. Beyond the shopfront and its attendant tables, the footpath opened up into the store's car park, where the side door was blocked off by three huge iron skip-bins piled with stock considered too worthless to put out for picking through.

Alongside the skips, rows of blistered bookcases and cabinets waited for the empty ribs of their shelves to be filled once more; back behind them, a house attached to the shop had its porch stuffed with hundreds more trinkets, and Colin supposed the owners of Mercury's Hoard lived there, for a sour yellow light shone through the pebbled glass panel of its front door. He felt like a thief, half-expected someone to step out of that house and apprehend him for his trespasses.

Shaking off this notion, he traversed a narrow path through the junk that led to the shop's front door. He cupped one hand to the glass and peered in to see if this dramatic purge had cleared the store of its stock. What he could make out of the interior implied it had, leaving only stacks of steel shelves arranged into odd, angular cairns on the old carpet; the tall, spindly shapes that stood still as statues among the shadows must have been denuded displays, ready to receive fresh treasures and bear them up for inspection in another shop, another city.

Colin wandered back to the shopfront, where Jackie waited by the car with her arms full of old biscuit tins. "I can use these. Could you open the back door for me?"

He obliged, resting his hand on her shoulder for a brief fix of touch as she hurried past him and back to the plunder. Her keen curiosity and enthusiasm for things new and old was just one of the aspects of her that he loved, and he thrilled to think there was still so much to learn. Jackie had always been reticent to discuss her past, hinting only that she'd been treated like a trinket by whatever careless company she'd passed through before him, which left him fearing the worst—but surely there were good memories yet to share, and he was happy to ration them out over the years to come.

A pang of love quickened his pulse, brought a smile to his lips. Colin fished out his phone, opened the camera, and captured an instant: his mundane miracle, face unmade and hair unbrushed, dressed down and distracted as she crouched over a cardboard box that was falling to pieces around a collection of clamshell video cassette cases.

"What was that for?" Jackie threw him a quizzical look. No matter how many times he told her, she never seemed to realise her own true worth—but to be fair, he didn't recognise much of the value she claimed to see in him, either.

"You're a treasure amongst treasures," Colin said.

Jackie gave a sardonic laugh as she gestured around her. "Yeah, I'm second-hand goods. Used and discarded, like the night you met me. Just some old trash left out on the footpath, in the rain, for the vultures to pick over."

It was two winters ago that Colin had found Jackie's huddled, sobbing figure on the stoop of an abandoned shop as he made his way home from a Saturday night cult cinema screening. He'd offered her his coat against the rain, then some sympathetic company, and finally, a gentlemanly escort to the nearest taxi rank. In the early, uncertain days of their relationship, she'd sometimes accused him of swooping in during a vulnerable moment, a bargain hunter scenting a discounted deal—and though she'd long since retracted the remark, he still cringed at the thought that, no matter how honest and well-intentioned his actions, there may have been some truth to it. After all, would a Good Samaritan really have insisted she take his coat home and given her his number to ensure that she'd have to speak to him again? But she was hardly in a position to pass judgement on anyone's motivations that night, since she still hadn't told him how she'd come to be on that derelict stoop in the first place, or what exactly had left her so distraught.

"You're priceless, my love," he assured her. "One of a kind."

"Yeah, well, you won't get much when you decide you don't want me anymore and trade me in," Jackie grumbled.

"Never going to happen, Jacks."

"That's probably what someone thought when they bought this," she said, holding up a battered VHS copy of *Harry Potter and the Philosopher's Stone*. "Somebody loved this, once. But how many times can you see and hear and feel the same things before they get boring, and you decide you want something new?"

Colin was opening his mouth to point out that he'd promised her forever, but held his tongue when Jackie squealed in delight at the sight of *Aladdin*, a movie she'd loved as a child. Let her enjoy the moment; there'd be plenty of time for words of devotion later. The traffic lights glowed amber to urge caution as he passed her by, brushing his fingers against the soft fall of her hair, and went back to the skips.

The proprietors must have been reluctant to get rid of all this stuff—the curiosities they'd collected over the years had surely gained some sentimental value after sitting on their shelves for so long, and maybe they'd even come to feel like the stock was their own, the shop their home. They were clearly close to their work, since they lived right alongside the store; maybe the two buildings had cross-pollinated, spreading cast-off merchandise into their private rooms and personal keepsakes into the workplace.

Colin tried to call the Mercury's Hoard staff to mind but drew a blank—he mustn't have paid enough attention at the time, and he had the impression they'd not extended much to him, either.

He remembered walking through the doorway with Jackie, a bell announcing their presence to an empty counter; he recalled traversing the store's many narrow aisles and overladen rooms, often more interested in fondling his partner than the wares on offer; but he couldn't quite recall the person who'd sold him the paperbacks he'd picked up. Most likely he'd been too distracted to notice much about them, since those dog-eared Tessier, Wagner, and Ligotti tomes had each been worth a lot more than the six bucks he'd paid for them.

A lot of the detritus in the skips tonight was of a literary nature, though much less interesting than the volumes he'd found last time: colourless technical manuals for obscure cars and tools, broken-backed dictionaries whose lexicons had long been exceeded and outdated, rotting storybooks for children from a cheerful era when boys were boys, girls were wives-in-training, and golliwogs were considered acceptable. Some old furniture had found its way in here, too—busted lamps poked their lightbulb heads up above the rubble like dead ideas, and the patterns on the hides of sodden couches might have been embroidery or mould. All these objects had travelled so far across borders, thresholds, and decades, were bound for the tip, where their accumulated memories and meaning would rot unnoticed beneath countless tons of ephemeral refuse. A shame, but at least he and Jackie were here to rescue some small pieces of those abandoned pasts.

Caught up in contemplation, Colin jumped in his own skin when a sudden slap stung his rump. He mock-growled as Jackie swept by with a cheeky laugh, chased her up to the porch of the house alongside the shop, caught her in gentle hands. She giggled as he planted a noisy kiss on her temple and wriggled free of his arms, intent on her mission.

The portico provided better protection from the intermittent rain, and here some more perishable items were displayed. A rolling rack was hung with coats and jackets and scarves and shirts, its motley rainbow muted by the night; a dresser held boxes of CDs, cut-price classical performances mixed in with one-hit wonders whose stars had waned even faster than they'd waxed; a wooden trunk was filled with shoes and boots and slippers and thongs, its lid thrown back like the mouth of an old clam hungry for leather and rubber. Jackie sorted through some assorted kipple as Colin poked at a stack of gardening and cooking magazines and then moved on to a plastic tub filled with DVDs. He was perusing these in search of anything interesting when Jackie pried a box out of a pile of random objects and waved it at him.

"Hey, babe! This looks like your kind of thing."

MAGIC TRICKS! The words floated in a speech bubble beside the head of a stage magician dressed in the standard top hat and cape, waving his wand as if to ensorcell anyone who might pick up the box. AMAZE YOUR FRIENDS! DISAPPEAR BEFORE THEIR VERY EYES!

Colin thought that would be more Jackie's jam—after all, she'd suddenly appeared in his life without explanation two years ago, and he sometimes feared she might mysteriously vanish just as quickly— but his interest was piqued. He took the slim cardboard container from her, wondering who had once been entranced by these tricks and why they'd eventually tired of them enough to cast them away.

Jackie was all about such thoughts. She believed that preowned goods carried more weight than new ones, as if they'd absorbed history on their way to her—some essence of their environments, some piece of the person who'd passed them on—and since meeting her, he'd reassessed the second-hand books that cluttered his shelves, had pictured strange fingers turning those pages and leaving behind microscopic traces of themselves like an invisible signature. Jackie had shown him the system was backwards, that used items were worth *more*—they had a past, had grown a soul. Like the people who took them and gave them away, every object was unique in the sum total of its experience.

"Good call. I'm putting this in the car. Anything you want me to take back for you?"

"Nah," Jackie replied, flicking through assorted clothes hung on the rickety rack like discarded skins. "I'm not done, though. I'll be here for ages yet."

"Back in a minute, then," Colin said, his voice ringing too loud in the post-midnight silence, and his eyes returned to the front door of the house attached to the shop.

They were now standing on its porch, the entrance only a couple of metres away, and since the door's glass panel was glowing a soft and sickly yellow, he had to assume someone was awake and able to hear their conversation. Mundane as their words were, he didn't like the idea of strangers being privy to his and Jackie's exchanges—didn't like that the door was slightly ajar when he was sure it had been closed the last time he looked. If there was further bric-a-brac to be browsed within the house, surely they'd have put up a sign to say so, or left the door open wider to show what the pebbled panel was keeping obscured. All Colin could see was a hint of homely floral-patterned wallpaper, and a thin, crowned shadow on the glass that might have been thrown by a tall, many-pronged coat rack.

Colin turned his back on the door and left the porch. He passed by the rows of cabinets on his way through the crowded car park, ducking around one that stuck out a drawer like a wooden tongue, and then the overflowing skips. He frowned when he reached his car and saw that Jackie had left the back door open, thinking it lucky there were no passers-by around to take an interest in its contents. Imagine that, the rummagers being rummaged—or, he idly fancied, perhaps he would find the back seat now filled with goods that neither of them had put in, vinyl records and ceramic plates and tin signs and plastic fast-food trinkets, as if the abandoned stock had seen an opportunity to flee to a new life and packed itself into the car while he wasn't looking. Colin saw no stowaways when he dropped the box of **MAGIC TRICKS!** onto the seat, but he made sure to close the door before turning back. No cars waited at the T-junction, but the traffic lights glared at him with red eyes regardless.

That brought a little more of his last visit to mind. He couldn't recall the face of whoever had served him, but he remembered their eyes—not glaring but staring in speculation, and not at him but rather the woman by his side. As he fished in his wallet for spare change, he'd idly imagined the clerk making him an offer of a good price to take Jackie off his hands. The random morbid thought had amused him in the carefree light of day, appalled him now that all was dark and his partner out of sight.

He couldn't see Jackie anywhere as he returned to the porch. He assumed that was because the light inside the house had now been extinguished, and neither the moon nor the streetlamps extended much illumination into that darkened portico—but when he stepped into the vestibule himself, he found himself alone among the stacks of knick-knackery. The only movement came from that rack of clothing, one coat near the middle swaying gently on its hanger as if waving a long-sleeved arm at him.

"Jackie?"

She wasn't among the cases and cabinets, either. Colin frowned as he stalked back to the road, casting a concerned gaze in either direction. No-one walked the footpaths, and he'd have heard if any vehicles had pulled up. He checked his car even though he knew it was ridiculous, and it was just the way he'd left it moments ago.

Colin reached into his pocket and caressed his phone with an anxious thumb as he hurried back past the skips, wondering if Jackie was playing a prank on him. It wouldn't be entirely out of character for her to be hiding somewhere amongst all this junk, waiting to leap out and startle him as he passed by. He kept a close eye on every shadow as he went back to the porch, but no ambush was forthcoming. If she hadn't strolled off for no apparent reason, and wasn't hiding amidst the bric-a-brac, where else could she have gone?

He turned a more critical eye on the house. Not only had the light been turned out, but the door had been pulled to and latched. Had she gone in there, then, thinking it might be another display area? Unlikely—and even if she had, why would the light have been put out? The idea sat heavy and awkward in his gut, gave him queasy visions of Jackie's characteristic curiosity leading her closer to the house's open mouth, of a lurking *something* pulling her swiftly inside before the door clicked shut and the yellow glow beyond dimmed into deepest dark.

Telling himself his imagination had been infected by all the horror fiction he read, Colin called Jackie's name once more as he pulled up her number on his phone. There was no reply from her voice, and for a second, none from the handset. Then he heard his call go through, heard her mobile begin to ring—in his ear from the speaker of his own phone, and also from somewhere within the shadows of the porch.

Confused, Colin used the light of his screen to pick out the contents of the nearest table. Jackie's ringtone was coming from somewhere amongst the trinkets and trumpery piled up behind the boxes of CDs, and its cheery melody—Lionel Richie's "Hello"—was eerily incongruous in this setting. If this was a joke then it was in exceedingly poor taste, and Colin's gut twinged in unease as he lifted framed sunset photos overlaid with Bible quotes, shifted aside chipped vases, cleared a pack of headless ceramic cats. Underneath it all, a slim black shadow cast a dim glow through its closed cover, and that glow died along with the cheesy ringtone as Colin ended his call and picked up Jackie's phone. The cover was dusty and scuffed, as though it had been sitting there undiscovered at the bottom of that pile of gimcracks for many months.

"Jacks? This isn't funny," Colin called, and his gut agreed that it really was not, that this was no prank. But then he recalled how that coat had twitched a sleeve at him when he returned to the porch, even though there was no breeze to speak of, and he spun back to the clothes rack with a gasp of revelatory triumph. He grabbed its metal frame and pulled it to one side, ready to cry out in discovery. Behind it, he saw nothing but the wall of the house.

Hissing a worried curse, Colin pushed the clothes rack back to its previous position and grabbed the long black sleeve that had waved at him. The empty arm was velvet-soft, all too familiar beneath his fingers. He shoved the other hangers aside and saw, in the scant light, that the coat was just what he'd thought it was—an old bargain once liberated from the Salvation Army, as recognisable as the body that had filled it a hundred times.

It couldn't be that one, though. There had to be countless such coats hung on charity shop racks all across town—the darkness was making a fool of him, playing into his deepest unreasoning fears.

Colin dragged the next hanger along, saw that it was filling the shoulders of a faded *Adventure Time* T-shirt, and the breath sucked from his lungs.

He stepped back from the rack, the chill night air spreading inside his chest. His eyes fell on the open trunk of shoes, and there, on top of the pile, sat an empty boot that bore a familiar pattern of yellow paint spatters on its toe.

"Jackie!"

The dark door watched him with a blank glass eye, blandly professing a silent innocence, and at once Colin was sure she was somewhere behind it. He jerked into motion and strode forward, raised a fist, rapped on the wood. That wasn't action enough, so he grabbed the handle. He expected resistance, and so was surprised when the brass knob twisted in his hand. Concern and fear swelled in his heart as he turned the handle and pushed the door wide.

Colin stepped through into the house, and his urgent stride faltered to a halt at once. No cosy hall waited behind the door, no homely floral-patterned wallpaper, no *walls*—just a vast vacant space disappearing into distant shadows, dark and deserted like a derelict warehouse. Bare cement gritted beneath his shoes, spotted here and there with discarded rubbish, and shafts of moon-glow poured in through unseen apertures in the ceiling. The house was an empty shell, bereft of light fixtures and furniture and any sign that life had ever flourished here.

Colin moaned her name once more, a mocking echo of his despair bouncing back at him from distant corners. Then he staggered back outside, cast his desperate gaze once more across the rows of bookcases even though he knew he wouldn't find what he sought. He pushed his way through to the shop door, peered a second time through the cool glass, and saw that those strange arrangements of stacked shelving had vanished along with the still shapes that had stood back in the shadows. The store was as empty as the house beside it. Mercury's Hoard had moved on.

Stunned by the abrupt disappearance he'd always feared but never expected, bereft of explanations, Colin walked on unsteady legs around the large skip bins and the once-valuable rubbish heaped within until he reached his car, an island of familiarity in a world that had turned strange and hostile in a heartbeat. The biscuit tins Jackie had gathered still sat in the back seat alongside a VHS copy of *Aladdin*, assuring him he hadn't imagined that or anything else. He turned to the shopfront with its signs both old and new—STILL SNAPPING UP SELECTED TREASURES—and spotted a small, familiar shape near the edge of the closest trestle table. He scooped it up into his palm with a gasp, certain he could feel a hint of warmth where Jackie's hand had wrapped around it.

Colin clutched the *Yellow Submarine* badge until its blunt edges cut into his palm and he fell back against the car, staggered by this sudden loss. The tangerine glow of the streetlights shimmered up at him from puddles in the road as rain began once again to fall,

192

and not only from the sky. He remembered it had been raining the night they met, and the tears came hot and hard.

His last words to her had been so mundane—*back in a minute, then*. Already he knew he would be forever haunted by the lack of a final *goodbye* or *I love you*, even a simple look or touch to let Jackie know just how much she meant to him—his treasure among treasures, one of a kind, the ultimate collectable. His heart tore open to admit the unbearable darkness, and behind him, the traffic lights once more completed their cycle of green to amber to red: *go, going, gone*.

About the Author:

Matthew R. Davis is an author and musician based in Adelaide, South Australia (Kaurna Meyunna Yerta). He's been shortlisted for a Shirley Jackson Award, the WSFA Small Press Award, and multiple Aurealis and Australian Shadows Awards, winning two Shadows for 2019. His books include *If Only Tonight We Could Sleep* (horror collection, Things in the Well, 2020), *Midnight in the Chapel of Love* (novel, JournalStone, 2021), *The Dark Matter of Natasha* (novella, Grey Matter Press, 2022), and *Bites Eyes: 13 Macabre Morsels* (flash chapbook, Brain Jar Press, 2023). He plays bass and sings in heavy bands, performs occasional spoken word, dabbles in short film, video clips, and graphic design, and loves to explore abandoned locations and second-hand stores with his photographer partner, Meg . . . such as the one that inspired "Trash and Treasure". (This tale is a warped account of their late-night visit to the closed Cross Road Collectables on September 1, 2018, and was written the following day. Its grief and fear of loss presaged their increasingly inevitable breakup a month later—but real life got a happier ending than the story.) Find out more at matthewrdavisfiction.wordpress.com.

Off the coast of Western Australia lies Penguin Island, where the damage done by an invasive monster is starkly visible.

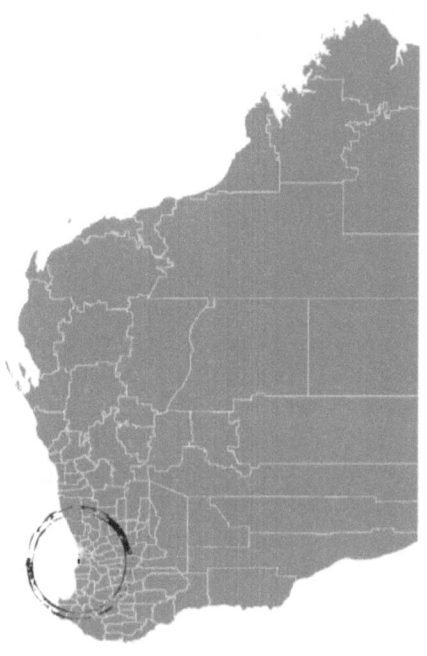

LOVE TO TRAVEL LOCAL

Emma Louise Gill

To: Jeanine Grey, AssistantEd

From: Adelaide Smith, Ed

Sol_System_Earth date: Monday 16th July 2035

FWD: Guest Post Submission: Love to Travel Local / Sol System / Earth / Australia

Jeanine. Happy (?) Monday. We've got a new Harry review; better take it on. A.

Begin forwarded message–

To: Love to Travel Local: The Milky Way's Honest Travel Blog.

Subject: Guest Post Submission: Love to Travel Local / Sol System / Earth / Australia

Sol_System_Earth date: Friday 13th July 2035

Author: H191M 'Harry' (they/them)

Dear Adelaide,

Please find below my fourth report from our Australian endeavour. Sponsors and links are indicated, plus images in attachments. I am requesting a backup portal for my next trip, though; don't want to get stuck on a rock for three days talking to ghosts again, haha. As a token of appreciation, samples of the sauce products mentioned are on the way.

See you soon,

H.

Harry (they/them), Sauce Maestrix Extraordinaire

Harry's Galactic Sauce

Contact: Saucy_Maestrix@HGSEnterprises.BelNet.AGal

—

Little Penguins, Likeable Squatters, and Less-Than-Impressed Sea Lions

By Harry of *Harry's Galactic Taste*, Platinum-Starred Traveller, Entrepreneur, and Sauce Maestrix Extraordinaire

Readers, the first thing to remember when visiting Penguin Island—a slab of rock 700 metres offshore from Rockingham, Western Australia—is to hang on to your portal! I made the mistake of photographing my new JustGoPortaPortal™ on the jetty, and in a moment of distraction (by a gigantic bird[1]) a human youngling took a fancy to its purple-toy-cat disguise and made off with it onto a departing ferry before retrieval was possible. Admittedly, not the best start—though far from my worst[2], and the

---

[1] *Pelicanus conspicillatus* is large enough to swallow a Grocular. Beware.

[2] You might recall, my first step onto the tarred sands of Hellenia accidentally crushed a squark which turned out to be their High Priestess, but I mended sacrilegious fences and Hellenia is now my biggest importer of Harry's Oops Sauce (containing essence of blasphemy, strong caution suggested). A stolen portal is a minor stumble by contrast.

portal was later recovered successfully from a 'Maccas' (a human provisions store).

Before that, however, I explored Penguin Island: a curious place of scrubby nature viewed from human-built platforms above low hillocks. My X-900iTerra scanner logged nineteen seabird species, indo-pacific bottlenose dolphins, and a rare 'Australian sea lion'—whom engaged in angry discourse over humans misnaming their own rocky prominence, 'Seal' Island. I recommend avoiding the subject, if you are lucky enough to meet such a creature.

Of course, I did not seek to commune with the dolphins, as per Galactic Legislation 3195.5: Discourse with Planet-Bound Ancestors—Cetaceans. It was both magnificent to witness their sleek forms in the wild ocean from which they evolved, and yet also like catching your parental figure stripped of garments serenading the stars while drunk on Martian wine[3]. A . . . memorable experience.

Moving on.

Penguin Island, while once inhabited by Noongar peoples, was largely left alone until a century ago when a white man took up squatting there. Nicknamed 'Seaforth', the McKenzie male blasted the limestone caves into habitable rooms, named them after British conventions, and crowned himself 'King'. Mainland settlers found his antics amusing; thus the government gave him a lease to rent the

---

[3] Mother One, if you are reading this: no, I have still not recovered.

land as a 'leisure facility', which he held for forty years[4]. Not much physical evidence now remains, but merrymaking ghosts reappear on occasion, among them the *particularly* loquacious and eccentric Seaforth.

For the interested amongst my readers: be sure to download alternative and historical dialects to your translators! I recommend SpeakEarthLikeANative and NotTheQueensEnglish.

In all, the place is a fascinating case study on how humans have 'claimed' land in the past two centuries. (Ironic, if you are keeping up with current events in the Sol System.)

As for the famed *Eudyptula* (little penguins): they inhabit the island and its marine surroundings, which are (barely) protected from interference. During my visit[5], the penguins were boisterous in their mating proclamations, squabbling over nest boxes. I spoke to one penguin in the Discovery Centre who told me their human-provided habitations were both welcome and hypocritical: "Giant scooping machines dig up the seabed, kill habitat, and break the food chain," he said (on condition of anonymity). "They've been doing it for years up and down the coast. Humans aren't content

---

[4] Reminds me of President Ix, a close personal friend of mine, whom I permitted to remain on the asteroid Jeronius Three in return for stewardship of Harry's Galactic Sauce factory. Seven hundred Standards later, our sauce is available across four galaxies. Never say no to useful squatters.

[5] Late June, the sixth month of the illogical and primitive Gregorian Calendar. Any system that requires additional days every four years needs serious revision.

with land. Want ocean, now. How will they live there? Breathe water? All that'll be left for us is *this*. How *nice*[6]."

The remaining penguins whom I approached were uninterested in discourse. Those that live in the Discovery Centre are unable to return to the wild due to ill health or age; they perform daily[7] for human tourists in return for shelter and food. Others on the island are skittish. Easily found by smell (beware your olfactory senses, readers!), their performances are restricted to the winter breeding season, when nest box cameras capture their lives. Human scientists study the population via numerous means[8].

Overall, I found the most fascinating aspect of Penguin Island to be the laughing human younglings on its beaches and lookouts, unattended by their device-hypnotised guardians. Their behaviour elicits an impression of freedom, in this place that humans consider 'wild'. Such ignorance as showcased here is subtle rather than blatant (unlike <u>elsewhere across Australia</u>). I bottled several samples. The palate, while sweet to start, has an emotional aftertaste that is bold and slightly sour.

Look out for the sauce at my next release: a limited run I call, '<u>Appropriation</u>.'

---

[6] Sarcasm. Humans cannot respirate dihydrogen monoxide, and I doubt the penguin meant 'nice' by dictionary definition. All visitors to Earth should familiarise themselves with such nuance of language. I reiterate my recommendation of the <u>SpeakEarthLikeANative</u> app. Use code HARRY20 for 20% off a Standard subscription.

[7] Not recommended viewing.

[8] Beware: do not engage scientists in conversation—they will tell you more than you ever want to know about scat, statistics, and the struggle for funding.

Happy travels,

Harry

Harry (they/them)

Sauce Maestrix Extraordinaire

Harry's Galactic Sauce

Attachments: IMG_1277xii–IMG_1491xvi

—

Jeanine,

Harry mentioned several negatives about their trip. Log a work request for surveillance/question RE: visitor compatibility at this venue ASAP. If satisfactory, still make sure to mention the 'Earth-Wide Travel HelpLine is complementary with all tickets' part at the bottom of H's post (but don't link to us directly; Keith just resigned. Actually, in regards to that—need a new translator ASAP. My Human is terrible. No, don't *use one of Harry's suggestions.)*

PS: When is my next meeting with Harry? I saw the word "soon" in their message. Just in case, better order another reinforced, triple-locking, thermal storage crate. I'm running out of space for the sauce samples. A.

Adelaide Smith, Editor-in-Chief, Kxc, JjMS, BBa, etc.

Long Arm: Sol Department

Contact: don't bother. Message my assistant(s) instead. If you can't find their contacts, you're not looking hard enough.

—

END

About the Author:

Emma Louise Gill is a British-Australian speculative fiction writer and coffee addict, living on Gnaala Karla Booja. Her short stories appear in AntipodeanSF, Crow & Cross Keys, Curiouser Magazine, Etherea Magazine, and others.

She blogs at emmalouisegill.com and procrastinates on Twitter @emmagillwriter.

Western Australia is home to Dugites, the Mulga Snake, the Western Tiger Snake, and the Goldfields Pipeline, a steel snake from Mundaring to Kalgoorlie.

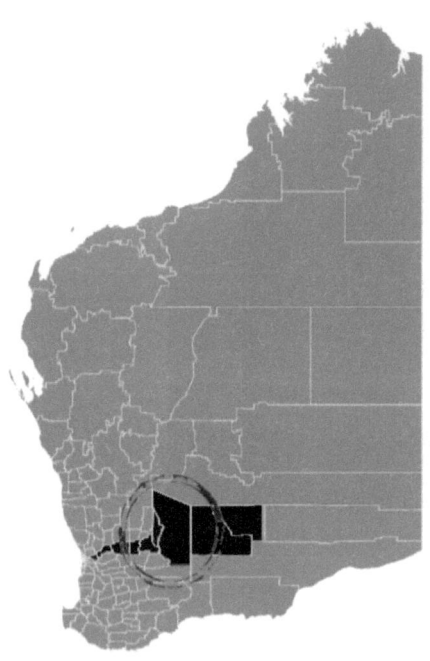

FOLLOW THE WATER

J. Palmer

The girl heard it first. A kind of dull reverberation from deep within something. *Dom, dom, dom.* A primordial heartbeat that existed ungoverned by the natural soundscape, which—until that moment—had been only the crack of thunder and the slap of hard rain. She pulled herself to a sitting position, shivering and hugging her arms against her saturated clothes. Next to her, the boy remained still. His ability to sleep through anything was a constant source of envy. She realised that she'd moved closer to him in the night—for warmth, she told herself—and wiggled away so that they were no longer touching.

A low, rumbling thunder rolled over the hill. She tracked it across the slate-coloured sky, and it left her staring at the Mundaring weir, miraculously still intact and now, even more incredibly, filled to the brim with water. *Dom, dom.* The sound came again. She hadn't dreamed it; it was not another echo of the week-long storm. Hauling herself to her feet, she tiptoed down through the sodden bush, her bones and joints aching despite her youth, until she reached the water's edge. She dropped to her knees to lap a day's worth with her hand, and this time, the noise was a kind of sucking, gurgling draw, like a plug pulled from an immense bathtub.

It eddied through the water and although she couldn't feel it, she imagined the vibration in her hand. Her next thought materialised behind her in a raspy voice.

"Someone's started the pipeline again."

She turned to face the boy, her nerves jangled by his silent approach.

He stood on the sandy waterline like a kangaroo trying to blend into the bush. "The pipeline," he repeated, this time pointing to the gargantuan wall of stone that was keeping the rain locked into the weir. "It's sucking up the water."

Dom, dom.

"That's impossible," she croaked back. "Someone has to work the pumps. It doesn't run itself."

"I know that." His eyes were glassy with sleep and nightmare.

The girl looked again at the wall; at the crumbling stone, the dilapidated viewing pagoda; at the valley around them, their exclusive purview for years now, since the world had disappeared. Since Perth had emptied in such ghastly exodus, leaving nothing but rotting metal skyscrapers and cracked, weed-claimed roads. Across from her, on the other side of the dam, lay the pipe itself. As thick as a fallen tree, it snaked out of the bush to submerge itself in the water where it slurped the stuff from the silty bottom. She tried not to picture the mouth of the thing, which surely existed at both of its ends. Two heads that would never meet. *Dom, dom.* It spoke to her from where it lay hidden in the depths, and she ripped her hand from the water.

"Someone's working the pumps," she said more to herself than the boy.

He nodded as she landed on the implication. "Someone's still out there."

* * *

The rain started again as they scrambled down to the first pumping station. It slicked the treacherous walkway, weaponising the dank weeds and soil that had been washed off the hill. They arrived hand in hand at the locked iron grate, hanging off each other so that if one of them slipped, there'd be no slack to allow a nasty fall. There was no one to call for help, no one to mend a broken ankle. The boy shook the door and the rattle bounced off the dam wall looming behind them.

"It can't be this pump," the girl said to his back. "We'd have heard it a mile away if it was." He ignored her to continue his fight with the door, which of course he lost. Hunger had made him weak, and despite having had no one to maintain the place in many years, the lock remained tight.

She stood next to him—intimately close, demanding his attention. "That means that whoever is running it, they're way down the pipeline. In the wheatbelt, maybe. At one of the pumping houses. I don't remember where they are. Merredin, I think? Or Coolgardie?"

"It could be anywhere. Maybe all the way at the other end. In Kalgoorlie."

She nodded, *yes*. "Either way . . ."

"Someone's still out there."

* * *

They drew a line in the wet soil and placed rocks on either side to represent pros and cons; a childish diagram in the dirt that they both blushed at, despite there being no one to witness it.

"So, if there are still other people alive, that's a good thing. Right?" He placed his stone before she could respond.

She removed it and dropped it on the other side of the line. "And what if they're cannibals? Rapists? Slavers? We don't even know why everyone left, let alone what they've been doing this whole time. And that's *if* it's even people running this thing."

He stared at her, dumbfounded. "What else would they be? Monsters? The pipeline is there for water. People need water. And this isn't a movie. People look after other people."

"Not always." She stopped short of explaining what she'd meant by the implied *monsters*. He could be so literal, sometimes.

"Fine," he said. "Pro. We're running out of food here anyway. Birds and 'roos are too hard to catch, and anything slow enough to get a hold of is drying up. I don't know about you, but flowers and ants don't exactly keep me going from dawn to dusk." As if to punctuate the statement, his stomach gave a painful rumble. He dropped the second rock.

"Con," she returned. "We haven't been outside this valley in a long, long time. You think there's not enough food here? Maybe out there, there's nothing. And this rain won't last forever. It's the middle of summer. We go marching along that pipeline and we *don't* find food and water, never mind people, we're screwed." She threw her own stone, equalising the diagram.

They continued in this tennis match for some time, oblivious to the endless rain, the divide of opinion as clear as the ugly divide in the dirt. The discourse backlit by the steady *dom, dom.*

Exhausted and somewhat defeated, the boy said, "I'm tired of being alone. Of us being alone, I mean. We need to find other people. And even if we don't find them, we need to know that we tried." He waited for her to meet his eyes. It was a long time coming. "This . . . thing that we do here. It's survival, sure, but that's all it is. It isn't life. It isn't natural."

She didn't respond, and they both found themselves staring at the rocks on the ground between them. A gust of wind brought a violent downpour, distorting and then erasing their crude plans on the floor. When the girl shivered again and still did not speak, the boy knew the decision had been made. "We go?"

The girl's reply was quiet, lost in the storm. "We go."

* * *

It would take a little under a month to walk the mammoth distance along the line, if indeed it was the terminus, Kalgoorlie, from where the water was being drawn. With their decision made and perhaps

207

fearful of the wedge driven between them, neither the boy nor the girl spoke or even thought much about the gargantuan scale of the plan. It wasn't until they finished their second day of marching that the ludicrousness of it all—the impossibility of what they were doing—became obvious.

The boy collapsed with his back to the pipe, hiding from the sun and aching all over. The girl spent some seconds scanning the horizon until, seeing nothing, she sat down next to him. Neither spoke for a long time. They concentrated instead on their blistered feet and parched throats, the dryness of which overrode all hunger. They'd passed by pumping station number two in Chidlow on their first day; had drunk from abandoned swimming pools, gritting their teeth to filter out the other life forms which clung to it. The rotting town had provided several plastic bottles which they filled and sealed, as well as one or two tins of food sitting dust-covered in abandoned kitchens—food which they would not risk eating until catching bobtail lizards and unlucky birds was no longer enough.

Station number three in Wundowie had been a similar experience, only with crippling exhaustion weighing them down, and they'd fallen asleep in the cobwebbed little shed housing the apparatus. The dying remnants of the westerly breeze had chilled their bones where it broke through the slats of the pump's housing. They dreamed of empty roads and empty skies; of the glistening reptile they were following, whose father had shot himself dead after the pressure of building such a thing or perhaps out of shame at producing the abomination still attempting its mournful parlay. *Dom. Dom.*

The dramatic rise of topography between Wundowie and pumping station number three had thrown them. The pipeline straddled the escarpment with lazy ease, belying the treacherous route they'd been forced to scramble over in order to follow it. The bush had closed in tight around them, halving their speed as they'd pushed through thick grass as tall as a man and stumbled through hidden dykes and undulating rock bed. It hadn't been two days since the last rains, but already the native flora had turned dry and papery, as though it preferred being that way. They'd surmounted the scarp at last, branch-scratched and thirsty, and now couldn't help but feel they'd been dealt a mortal blow.

"We can't stay here tonight," said the girl. Her voice was croaky with thirst, her lips caked with bone-dry saliva. She didn't need to add the contradictory fact—the boy knew it just as well.

"I don't even know where the next pumping station is. It could be a hundred kilometres. Look at how the pipe slopes down from here. You don't need a pump to send water that way. Gravity does it all." He shook his head, reaching up and stroking the steel behind him, as though suing for peace with the thing. "We won't make it today."

"Maybe we could rest here for now, and keep going at night. It's only going to get hotter from here on out." She reached into her tattered backpack and produced a bottle of sepia water. "This is the last of it, until we find more." She put it back without drinking.

"You want to stumble along this thing in pitch darkness?" asked the boy. "If one of us breaks a leg, that's it, we're done. We're ant food."

"We can walk along the top. Carefully," she added, before he could argue. "Look at you. You're already burned to a crisp."

This he couldn't refute, and he shut his eyes instead. The heavy pulse of the line drummed against his skull. *Dom. Dom.* He didn't hear the girl say to him, "Stay here. I'm going to try catching some food," and he didn't wake up until she returned with the sun setting behind her, a limp bobtail hanging from one hand. He hauled himself to his feet, allowed a tiny smile at her.

She smiled back. "I'm going to clean it. See if you can get a fire happening."

The boy was crouching over the little mass of kindling, rubbing his hands raw on the improvised ferro rod when, in his periphery, the girl leaped back from the bag containing their knife. Her startled yelp broke the silence of the hill like a blasphemy. He reached her in time to see a muscular brown shape disappear back inside the rucksack. "Did it bite you?"

She shook her head, vigorous with adrenalin. "Just scared the hell out of me."

"It's in the bag."

"I know!"

"So, we need to get rid of it."

She gestured sarcastically. "Be my guest."

Biting his lip, the boy tiptoed to the bag, leaning forward as far as possible to reach it. He wrapped his hand around a strap and gave it a tug; the coiled shape within stirred but otherwise remained still. Cursing under his breath, he tried once more and then, when the snake still hadn't budged, sucked in a desperate breath and hoisted the entire thing off the ground. The girl yelped again and the boy released the bag in mid-air, darting backward and out of the drop zone. The snake and the bag separated in-flight–a terrifying display of serpentine anger–and the animal landed with a chilling, weighty thump. It slithered in a ferocious circle, carving shapes in the dirt that made the girl think of her Grandma's paintings, then, having spotted the boy, made an angry line straight for him. He lashed out with his foot—an inelegant and clumsy soccer kick—and the snake reared backward with a hiss before disappearing into the grass.

The two of them stood in shocked silence, wary of disturbing the thing should it still be waiting there in the scrub, preparing its moment. At last, the boy found his voice. "Walk on top. At night."

The girl nodded. "Walk on top."

* * *

He wouldn't admit it, but the boy was glad to have switched to night-time travel. His skin had indeed been scorched red by the sun. He was sure the girl had suffered too, although whatever damage had been done was not so visible or obvious. They adjusted quickly to walking by moonlight, and they made good progress with the *tap tap* of their feet combining with the *dom, dom* of the pipe, a metronome by which they crossed to the next pumping station.

When that rhythm faltered, they knew something was wrong. The pipe's heartbeat grew limp and was replaced by a noise that at first sounded like a gale skimming the wheat-logged fields all around them. They soon realised it was the roar of water. An odd hour or so where the ground around the pipe shimmered in the nocturnal glow before the situation became apparent.

The pipe was leaking. No, not just leaking. Water was cascading out of the pumping house with the force of a cleaved artery. With no one to collect it and nowhere to go, the precious stuff was pooling along the structure, and by the time the boy had leaped down into it, shin-deep (the girl hissing at his foolhardiness), it was obvious that a valve had been opened or had broken. Hammering himself against the pump house door, water sloshing around his legs, he failed to hear the girl's warning, and she jumped down after him to repeat it.

"I said, what the hell are you doing?"

"What does it look like?" he yelled back. He kicked at the door, but being so submerged, failed to generate serious power.

The girl grabbed him by the shoulders and pulled back with remarkable strength. They unbalanced together. "Stop! Oh my God, *stop* and think, would you?"

"We can't just leave it leaking like this! It might be days before someone gets here to fix it. Weeks, even. If someone's gone to the effort of getting the thing working again, out in Kal, for God's sake, don't you think they need it?"

"That's exactly my point. If we fix it, or turn it off, or whatever, they're going to know someone was here. They'll know about us."

"And? I thought that was why we were doing this?"

She began a response, and then stopped. Instinctively, she pulled her arms into the sleeves of her jacket, hiding her wrists. An action he'd seen before.

"Okay", he said. "You're right. We don't know who these people are or what they want, or if they're . . . the wrong kind of people. We need to be careful. But we can't leave the water running."

She nodded. "I know."

The boy stood for a moment, reading her face. The water continued its gurgling cacophony. "Let's see if we can close it off, then make a beeline up the pipe. If we keep it between us and the road . . . we should be able to hear anyone who comes to see what happened. Or at least, they won't be able to see us. Okay?"

"Yeah . . . okay."

213

They knocked the door in together; it shuddered under the dual assault, and the lock splintered in a shower of flaky copper. Inside wasn't much more than a thick iron wheel mounted on a U-bend pipe, and after several minutes grappling with it with water up to their thighs, the din outside quietened to a soft trickle. A long moan shuddered down the length of the pipe and disappeared into the distance. A few seconds later, the *dom, dom* had returned.

The girl was wading to the door before the boy could say anything. "Let's go. Quickly."

He followed her over to the pipeline. She was already feeling her way along the thing, looking for a space where they could cross; even outside, the water was at such a level that squeezing through the miniscule gap beneath it would risk drowning. She continued to harry him, panic welling within her at the thought of being found. Despite his relative optimism, the boy couldn't help but feel a little anxious himself as they passed the valve that the water had been spewing from. The girl threw him a look, and she did not need to explain the implication.

Someone had opened the valve. And perhaps they'd done it to see who would close it again.

* * *

They managed to get over the pipeline after scrambling up one of the concrete brackets that held it in place, the boy at first shoving the girl upwards who then turned to hoist him after her—a simple process for a pair as youthful as they, made next to impossible by exhaustion and their still wet hands slipping on the smooth construction of the thing. They walked (staggered) along its length, right hands brushing the pipe as though they were afraid to lose it in the red-smeared scrub that stretched all around them, their bottles filled with earthen and grainy water scooped from the flooded pump station. The *dom, dom* now back to its previous healthy timbre.

As before, the girl heard the new sound before the boy did. She threw her hand behind her to bring him to a stop, and then—before he could ask what she was hearing—she dragged him to the next bracket where they could lie undetected from the road on the other side of the pipe.

"What the hell are you doing?" the boy hissed as he fidgeted in the gravel.

"Listen!" the girl snapped back.

The boy strained his ears and was about to remonstrate further when he heard it. A second baseline was filling the void left by a world gone silent, backdropping the thrumming snake they'd been following. It chugged through the air, growing louder.

"It's a motorbike."

"Shh!"

The boy had wriggled flat onto his belly before she could stop him, digging his lank hair into the dirt to peek beneath the pipeline. "There's three of them . . ."

She couldn't help herself; she pressed herself into the ground, right up against the boy, to see for herself. "What are they doing?"

"I don't know . . . wait, look . . ."

"Oh my God . . ."

One of the bikes had turned around, throwing up a cloud of copper dust, obscuring the view of the riders. It roared back past the others, spraying gravel as it veered off-road, skirting as far into the shrub as it could without overturning.

"Jesus . . . we need to go . . ."

"No. Stay here." Her iron grip on his shoulder stunted the argument forming on his lips, and he obeyed the instruction. "They'll spot us if we run."

"Jesus . . . they're looking for us. They're fucking looking for us!"

"I know."

Another bike had roared around; the rider was probing his way toward the pipeline, wrangling the spitting, thumping machine in random directions, jetting forward on one wheel before veering away from a dyke or swathe of unpassable foliage. A third vehicle, a rust-chewed ute, had rolled to a stop on the road. Ungainly shapes writhed in the tray, contorting themselves against the ropes that lashed them together. The driver exited the cab to yell and beat them, and they stopped.

"Jesus . . . I'm sorry. I'm so sorry, I should have listened."

"Shh!"

The first grunting bike continued to probe toward the pipe, while the second returned to the road to scout back and forth in long, lazy loops. The boy and the girl buried their faces in the dusty ground, afraid now to even shift backward. Their hands were laced, fingers white-knuckled, as though to break the other's bones might tip some cosmic chain reaction—might make these men turn and leave and not come back.

They stayed that way for a long time, breathing straight into the dirt. The violent bleating of the motors ebbed in and out until eventually they softened and, after what seemed like a hundred torturous years, they faded back the way they'd came, heading toward Kalgoorlie.

Still the boy and the girl didn't dare move. They stayed locked in the conjoined pose of lizards compressing themselves into the sand, until the sun dipped, and the cold night re-affirmed its grip.

An hour later, they heard the screams.

* * *

They couldn't turn back. Even if the men hadn't roared through again, this time tripled in number and heading toward Perth, they hadn't the food and water supply to make what was, by now, a longer trip than pushing on to the end of the pipeline. Although the day had fallen silent, neither of them dared to stand upright as they limped along the far side of the pipe; they each remained hunched over, aching backs added to their litany of physical discomfort, sticking to each other like glue. They kept a constant

217

watch for water—a trickling culvert, a rain puddle, anything—but there was none. Eventually, the girl spoke.

"What do we do if we get there . . . and right now, that's a big if . . ." The boy shook his head, as though to dispel her pessimism despite the plentiful supporting evidence, but otherwise said nothing. "What if we get there and they're all like that? What they did to those people last night . . . If we . . ."

"I don't know," he snapped. He took several paces more, then stopped and turned, fearful to leave her even that far behind. "What do you want me to say? That we'll just walk all the way back to Mundaring? Pick up where we left off? Or that we'll skip Kalgoorlie and head right into the Nullarbor? Hell, maybe life is normal in Adelaide. We could walk all the way down to Esperance, huh? Sleep and fish on the beach? Jesus Christ . . ."

The girl made no attempt to dry her tears, although they ran down her face in admirable silence. "You always act like you know best. Like I'm an idiot who couldn't survive without you." She shoved her wrists toward him. The pose made her look like a scrawny, pathetic scarecrow. Her scars were visible even now, in the glaring mid-morning sun. "I was happy living at that stupid dam. I was happy when it was just you and me, and the bush and the sky, with no one else there to screw things up. I don't miss the world. I don't miss what used to happen to me, or the homes I got locked up in. You know what I did that night the world ended? I fucking cheered. I celebrated quietly in my bed, and when I woke up and *he* wasn't there anymore, I trashed the entire Goddamn house and ran into the bush."

The boy stood in shocked silence. Some bizarre pain was gripping his chest, his heart wheezing under a new strain. She'd never talked about her arms before. He'd seen them, but she'd never talked. He took a cursory glance behind him and then over to the empty road on the other side of the pipeline, barely registering the danger that it still posed. "When . . ."

"I was out there for *months* before you found me. And I was doing fine. *You* were the one who looked like you'd fly away in a breeze. Who'd made himself sick drinking un-boiled water and licking ants from the rocks. You came into my perfect world, and you didn't rescue me, I rescued *you*. Now look at us. We're stuck out here in the middle of nowhere, with cannibals searching for us on fucking motorbikes. We've got no food, no water . . ."

His response hit her like a slap in the face. "Turn back then."

"What?"

"If I ruined your life so bad, you shouldn't have come. Go back to Mundaring and live out your days in your beautiful little valley. Alone."

"It's too late to go back. You know that. God, you . . ."

He shrugged. An infuriating, unbothered shrug. "You say you got out of prison? Well, I got put into one that night. I'm sorry for what happened to you. I really am. But I had what you never did, and I lost it all when everything disappeared." He swept his hand down the length of the pipe, toward Kalgoorlie. "And I'm going to get it back again."

A small sound crept out of her lips; it made him stop and turn back.

"What?"

"You had it," she repeated. "With me. I mean . . . didn't you?"

He shrugged again. "I don't know. You tell me."

She didn't. She stood trembling in the burning sun, crisscrossed arms exposed to the world, with tidal waves of hurt and longing and she didn't know what else colliding inside of her. Not so much as a ripple on the surface. She stood there as silent and as invisible as she did in those tiny dark rooms, praying the men in the lounge or kitchen or wherever they'd be were passed out and would stay that way if she all but ceased to exist. She said nothing to the boy.

He shrugged again, said something she didn't hear, and continued down the pipeline. This time, she couldn't bring herself to follow him.

* * *

His head swirled as he marched through the heat. The drone and click of desert-hardened insects pressed in on him, claustrophobic and angry, while the scrubs rattled in a breeze that was hardly there. He walked until his face and neck and back were drenched in sweat, until he no longer registered the crunch of his feet on the gravel and no longer saw the point in looking behind him to see if she was coming, because he knew now that she wasn't.

With his brain pounding against his skull, he collapsed with his back to the pipe (*dom, dom)* and hung his face between his arms to shield it from the sun. The pipeline throbbed behind him, the force of the water pulsating through his raggedy form, while the insects of the dry, dry landscape doubled in volume.

Sitting there, with no thought of getting back up and continuing, or of finding food or water, but rather lost in thoughts of everything he should have said but didn't, he failed to hear the whisper of something long and muscular writhing beneath the pipe. And when he threw his head back in frustration at the world, and planted his hands firmly by each hip, it was as much a shock to him as it was the snake he'd pressed into the ground.

A sharp sting as it got its fangs into the meat of his palm—a reproachful hiss as he shook the thing off, panicked and filled with cold, nauseating adrenalin. By the time he'd scrambled to his feet it had bitten him again, lancing itself full-length to take hold of his ankle. He fell backward and scooped up a rock without looking. The snake lunged once more (he didn't feel the bite this time) and he brought the rock down hard. It pinned the serpent by its midsection, earning him another stinging strike as it coiled over on itself and attacked his wrist, and then at last he managed to catch the thing square on its head; it writhed and coiled, and after a second strike, went silent.

The boy sat there with blood speckled over his wrists and legs, breathing hard in wet, raspy drags. His heart hammered against

221

his ribs, and it wasn't long before his throat began to constrict on itself (like a python) and every exhale became a long, drawn-out labour. He staggered to his feet and continued walking in his original direction, more desperate than ever for water. *Dom, dom.*

Black spots filled his vision as the day waned, and every new flutter of leaves at his feet sounded to him like another dugite-the same dugite, maybe, that he'd evicted from the bag, although before now, he would have called that impossible-and by the time the sun had set properly, he was vomiting.

* * *

The girl stumbled back down the pipe. The thud of water being pumped past her had synchronized with her own pounding head, a combined symptom of her approaching dehydration and the anger bubbling into a foam within her. How could he have turned and left like that? As though ditching her was just another survival decision, as cold as smashing a lizard over the head or stealing chicks from a heartbroken magpie's nest. She'd given him everything, had been a dingo to his wobbly-legged poodle, ripping him back from the pathetic death that had awaited him. She'd given him something of a family when—at that point—he would never have had one again. And now he was gone, shedding her like a reptile sheds its skin, pursuing God knows what in Kalgoorlie when their life in Mundaring had been beautiful.

She walked on despite her protesting body, despite the searing thirst and the fire in her belly fueled by emptiness, tinned food all gone. She was powered solely by the need to move, to do something physical enough to stop her dwelling on what she'd lost. The obscene trumpet of an engine blared occasionally over the landscape, forcing her to drop to her hands and knees. When the sun slipped over the horizon ahead of her, she at last succumbed to exhaustion and wedged herself between the pipe and a trestle like an echidna in a pathetic, dirty nest. And when even the murky twilight disappeared, and the moon failed to materialise—when the entire world went black and silent—the loneliness hit her with the force of a freight train, the likes of which would never run again, and she realised the boy had been right.

Whatever it was she'd thought she hadn't needed, she'd had it with him; the entirety of family, friendship, and love, distilled to a single person and localized to that idyllic, peaceful valley. A valley that would now be intolerably empty, even if it were to bloom with rain and food and life forevermore. She would never have left, given the chance again, and given she could have convinced him to stay, but now, shivering in the dark with the pipe hammering right above her head, she knew what she had to do.

She wriggled herself out from under the thing, brushed the worst of the dirt from her clothes (or as much as she could tell in the barely-there light of the stars), and forced herself on a brisk march before her body could say otherwise.

"There's only two days total between us," she whispered. "And I'm faster than him."

She couldn't realise, then, how painfully true that was.

* * *

In her heady mix of exhaustion and fear, she almost passed right by him. He'd buried himself beneath the pipe to escape the burning sun, and as still as he was with his limbs askew, he seemed as much a part of the environment as the tube itself. She jumped when the image had processed, and then was on her knees trying to shake him awake. The details of his collapse-his reddened clothes, vomit stains the colour of a riverbed-danced in her peripheral thought, not forming a story.

He stirred at last but didn't open his eyes. Rather, he screwed them even tighter and groaned. The girl stopped shaking him.

"I'm here," she whispered. "It's okay. I'm here."

He reached out-got a hand on her shoulder and kept it there. "What happened?"

"Snake," he managed to groan. "It's still here . . ."

"No," she reassured him, filling herself with false confidence, hoping to ride the wave of it and keep ahead of the truth they both knew. "It's gone. Look." She leaned over to take hold of a long-dried stick and then beat the ground with it, sweeping the gravel around the pipe in a way that would frighten away any serpent, angry or not. He coughed and dribbled out what was more blood than saliva. The girl had retrieved the last of their

224

water from the bag and was unscrewing the lid when the boy waved his hand and almost knocked it from her grasp. He still hadn't opened his eyes; she could see now that they were swollen shut.

"Don't," he wheezed. "Don't waste it. You'll need it to get home."

The wave of confidence crashed, and the succeeding rip pulled the girl straight back the way she'd come, dragging her across the knowledge that she was never going to get home, that pushing on to Kalgoorlie was now her only option, and she'd be doing it alone.

"I'm sorry for making you do this," he drooled.

"You didn't." She shook her head, then remembering he couldn't see, cradled his face. "You didn't. I would have followed you anyway. I would have come with you."

"We shouldn't have left Mundaring. You were right. We had everything we needed." His voice was fading, following him into a sleep from which he'd never wake. Pathetic, dehydrated tears ran down the girl's cheeks, carving paths through the grime and dust that had caked there. "I only thought . . ." He disappeared beneath the tide of consciousness, then bobbed back to the surface. "I only . . . thought . . ."

She leant forward and pressed her forehead against his. "I know," she whispered. "You thought that we could share it with someone."

He didn't answer, but she kept on speaking. She pulled him closer and said to him things she'd never dared admit out loud. Things she'd held private since the day she'd found him and warmed his shivering body—since he'd wrapped her lacerated wrists with cloth torn from his own shirt—and by the time she'd finished her confessions, he was still and silent.

She remained in that position, a crouched embrace, and cried for hours until at last, drained of all energy, she lapsed into unwanted sleep. When she woke, she tucked the boy beneath the pipe, hoping in some way that it would protect him from the sun and the animals and anything else that might find him, and then she gathered the bag and set off in the direction of Kalgoorlie.

* * *

The final leg of the journey passed in a fever dream. Half numbed by grief, one foot in death's door with nothing left to give, she stumbled and shuffled her way along the pipe, its never-ending length now something of a comfort in the flat, arid landscape on the edge of the Nullarbor plain. The last of the water was long drunk, and she followed the pipe not only as a waypoint, but for the knowledge that somewhere up ahead it would disgorge the liquid for which her body ached.

She had only a perfunctory plan should she make it to Kalgoorlie. The odds of receiving a friendly welcome were next to nothing, but with the boy's death a painful absence in her heart, she kept his idea alive enough to push her forward those last excruciating miles. Only two items remained in the bag. One was a bundle of shrub leaves arranged in what passed for a bouquet, chosen for their saturated olive green against the dried sages and browns that flourished in the perpetual drought, and which, in her trauma-stricken mind, could make do as an arrival gift. The other was a long piece of bluestone taken from the railway line. She'd sharpened it against the pipe, timing her strikes to the now familiar thump of the water. It was not a weapon—not something that could give her hope against a rabble of armed, horrifyingly well-fed men. But she could use it quickly—knew which cuts to make—to ensure her journey would finish on her terms, and no one else's.

* * *

In the end, she used neither of the items. The pipe skirted the townsite proper, following the railway as it swerved around the crumbling colonial hall and the surrounding shells of former pubs. Caught on the outer side of it, she barely saw the town, and managed to cross the Northern side of it without being seen herself. And when she didn't come across any obvious opening—no sudden gap in cover where the pipe burrowed itself underground like a worm—she struggled to find any reason to climb the thing and approach whoever was living there. She had arrived at the place depleted, heartbroken, and empty of all reason or care to make contact with anything or anyone, no matter the potential risk or reward.

227

Deciding that all the connections in the world stripped down to a single relationship had been enough for her, she bypassed the town completely, listening to the improvised generators and voices carrying across the flat cityscape, and made her final, ragged steps up the slope to Mt. Charlotte, where the pipeline finished in ignominious fashion. With the moon basking the surroundings in a cold blue glow and the sharp rise of the of the abandoned open-cut mine in the middle distance, the girl traced the pipe's final segment to the reservoir. It spiraled up the pathetic hill—a mountain in name only, relative to the flatness that surrounded it—before coiling over the concrete basin. There at last, she spied the end of the thing-the second head-spewing its contents into the bucket the way the boy had spewed the last of his life into the gravel.

She dropped the bag on the cracked pathway, knowing she wouldn't need it anymore, and after hopping the little fence, lay face down on the grate so that she could watch the swirling water and the stars reflected therein.

What she would do in the morning—if indeed she woke up again—she didn't know, and didn't care. They'd set out on their journey to rejoin the fragmented family that had once made up the world, and in doing so, had fragmented their own tiny facsimile. At the same time, they'd solidified it—proven its mettle—which never would have happened had they stayed in their valley.

With the moon waxing over the sky in its silent arc, the girl closed her eyes and concentrated on the cool of the water beneath her, the warm caress of the easterly wind, and the comfort of knowing that it was still just him and her, and would be forever.

She made one last effort to hear the pipe—to listen to the *dom, dom*—but it was drowned by the gurgle of water arriving at its final destination, and then she was asleep.

About the Author

J. Palmer is a languages teacher and an Australian writer of speculative fiction. He grew up in the shire of Mundaring, where C.Y O'Connor's water pipeline begins, and he recently spent a year teaching in Kalgoorlie, where it ends after some 600km. In between all that, J. Palmer lived and worked in London for five years. He now resides on Wadandi Boodja (Dunsborough in Western Australia), where he teaches English and tolerable Japanese.

A few hours north of Perth are idyllic coastal retreats. But be warned, even the monsters need an escape now and then . . .

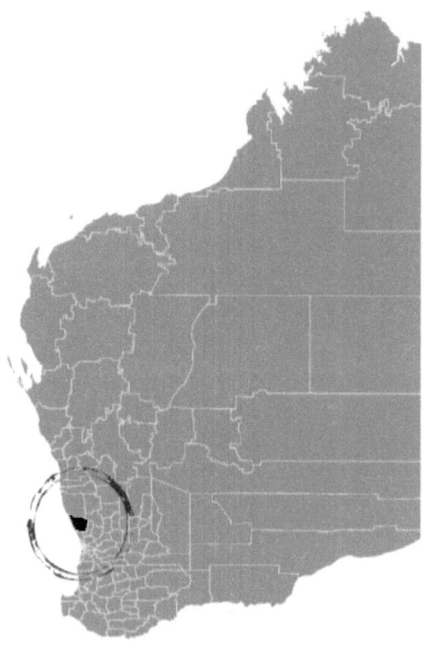

GOTHIC QUEEN

Jordyn Presley

Paula is woken by her Nan's voice echoing in her ears. The words
are indecipherable and leave her stomach churning and
somersaulting. Paula scrubs her face with her palms, kicking off
the twisted covers, finding it hard to shake the feeling that she isn't
alone as her phone starts ringing. Paula stubs her toe as she gets
up to answer it, scooping it up from the edge of her scratched
kitchen table. The unit is too small, but in Perth, affordable
rentals are hard to find. Luckily Paula knows someone who knew
someone else who could give her cheap rent until she is able to
work again. She is working on getting back on her feet.

"Is this Paula?" A gruff voice barks at her down the line.
Cigarette smoke drenches his breath as he coughs, waiting for her
reply.

"Who is this?"

"I'm the owner of your grandmother's building. I'm only new
to the job but got worried when the little old lady missed her rent
payment. Listen, there's no easy way to say this so I'll just get right
to the point. She's dead. I'm sorry."

Paula imagines this man on the other end of the line, stooped
over and sweating, playing with a ginger beard, cigarette burning his

hand as he makes this call. His face must be twisted in some awful, pitying expression as he waits for her answer. She cannot give it to him right now. He understands and lets her have a moment.

Paula is overwhelmed. She had only spoken to her nan less than a week ago. She was fine. Paula twirls her fingers in her black hair, pulling out a few strands, focusing on breathing. How had she missed this?

"Look, I know this is hard. Everything has been taken care of, well, almost everything. She had some great friends. I just need you to come and clean out her place. I got your number from the ladies at the op shop who worked with her. Can you come?"

Paula resists the urge to hang up, throw the phone away, stamp on it. She watches rain fall over the early morning traffic and imagines throwing her phone out of the boxed window. The blaring of horns and swearing of strangers is all muffled as if it is underwater. She has been to cities all over the country, has trekked through bushlands, waded through rivers, climbed mountains but it is time for her to go home now. She bites her nails. Crunch. Crack.

"Yes, I'll be on the next bus out."

"Great. I'm busy today so I won't be able to let you in. I need the place cleaned and ready for the next tenant by the end of the week. I know you have a key. Just leave it in my office or with a neighbour when you're done. We're all friends here."

He hangs up before Paula can, a fist forming inside of her body that pummels at the walls of her stomach. A grief storm. A rage.

This is not the way these things are handled. Her nan should have had more respect, her life worth more than the few dollars provided by the next tenant.

Alone in the unit, Paula digs the crust of sleep from her eyes and tries not to bawl like a baby. She has no one to call. Her nan would have known what to do.

Paula arrives at the bus stop two hours early, sick of the sight of her small unit and the silence. She gulps down overpriced water at a table in the corner, as far as possible from the terminals that fill up with disgruntled passengers, worn-out drivers and vehicles that spew black smoke into the air. It is too loud. She keeps her distance, back turned to the hustle and bustle. Her eyes are on the white tiles gone yellow with grime. She hates buses, this feeling nurtured and grown into fear since her mother boarded one and never came home, and can count the times she has taken a bus anywhere on one hand. Bracing herself against the table, she stands up. A wave of weakness pushes her back, chilling her core. Paula yearns for her nan now that she can't find her in the faces of strangers. Paula has been away from home for the past two years, but it might as well have been two decades. Now she is too late.

* * *

Arriving in one of the small Western Australian towns that hug the coast, several hours away from the bustling city of Perth, is a journey she would repeat a hundred times over. If only without this bus that smells like sweat and rotten banana. Paula never tires of seeing the icy blue water or the emerald mountains. Her nails have made bright red crescents in her palms.

Paula has dipped into her savings, hesitant to take this trip with so little money, but she needs to do this. Guilt worms its way up her stomach, threatening to overwhelm her. She waited too long to return. She had the money, once, but missed her chance. Now she finds herself paying for the bus and taxi fares she should have paid much sooner.

Why didn't you tell me you were sick? I would have been here. I should have been with you.

The taxi does not take long to arrive and the ride is silent. The driver hardly moves a muscle. Paula glues her face to the window, absorbing everything. The long, straight roads surrounded by sugar cane and banana crops. The endless blue sky. The sweltering heat. Winding down the window, she hopes for a cool breeze and is slapped in the face by more heat. Waves of sweat fall off her like tears. Wiping her hand over her forehead, Paula is glad to be in the back.

The town greets her in the same sleeping manner it always has, unchanged in all the time she has been away. The wide roads a sea of gravel. A few shops, busy pub, local kids running around, their parents watching from verandahs that are mottled grey and split by the heat. Surrounded by mountains, this town has hollowed its place in the world like a nest. For most, a stop on the way to another destination or to rest for a moment. Time slows down in this town. Paula is aware that the driver's eyes are on her, waiting for her to signal a stop. She does so, handing her the money and wishing her a safe trip home. Maybe she should have remembered her name, made it a little more personal. This trip is out of the way. Too late now. Paula's heart pounds as she steps into the heat and her silent companion drives off.

Paula walks up a small alley from the main road, following the worn concrete footsteps to where she grew up. A small, one-bedroom unit at the end of a line of identical cement buildings. Grey, drab, keep the cool in. Neighbours are running around inside, but the street is empty. Focusing on breathing through the heat, Paula grabs her key from her pocket, dangling the red clip from her forefinger. Sneaker catching the edge of the concrete, she trips and falls with a hard thump on the ground, head hitting a few loose pieces of gravel. Her head pounds, but after moving her limbs and inspecting herself, she is able to stand and realises she is not seriously hurt. Dusting herself off and touching her hairline, Paula notes that it is tender, scraped, and will bruise. She hurries to the purple door they painted when she turned twelve, covering themselves in just as much paint as the door. They looked like eggplants. It did not come out of her hair for weeks. She can still taste it. Putrid. Sticky.

Paula unlocks the door, pushing her way inside and shutting the door behind her before anyone can see her. Her head feels fuzzy, a cotton ball on her shoulders. She knows these people, they are lifers. They will never leave. She does not want their pity, their tears, having enough of her own; she will drown in theirs.

Paula flicks on the light and draws a shaky breath. The place smells like musky perfume. She exhales. It comes out as a groan. She bites her lip and screws her face up as a tear makes its way down her cheek, sinking into the floor. Searching for a tissue in the yellow kitchen cupboard, she pushes aside odd pieces of clothing and knick-knacks. A fairy drops to the floor and rolls under the fridge in a cloud of dark glitter, getting stuck by the door.

The room is hot and musty. Paula opens the two blinds, letting in light, and the windows, desperate for air. She can breathe a little easier now. The air is still, but the heat settles. It is not unbearable now, just familiar. Her nan loved packing material, keeping many boxes in a cupboard just in case they were needed. Paula laughs, then rubs her arms as a chill runs through the air. She is no longer sticky, she has grown used to the heat. She grew up with only a fan on the hottest days, seeking shelter underneath large trees or the local shops during real scorchers. This heat is nothing. Winter makes its way here, but it is a long journey and it does not stay for long.

Entering her nan's room, Paula screams. A young woman, dressed all in black, stands by the bed. Her delicate, doll-like features flicker like a static television, creating a blurred image that quickens Paula's pulse. *She can't be real.* Paula tries to blink away the impossible presence. The woman remains. She tilts her head to the side and moves towards Paula, who backs away and hits the wall. Paula looks beyond the woman and focuses on the chipped, blue paint of the wall, hoping this is some figment of her imagination.

"Come," the woman says in a lilting voice.

Paula shakes her head.

"Come." The voice is more forceful now. Paula does not react. The woman approaches Paula and touches her arm, sending a jolt through her. The impossible doll-woman's touch is soft. Paula shrinks further into the wall as her head pounds. The woman moves past her and stops, waiting. Paula has no choice. There is something familiar about her.

They leave the unit and follow the road to a nearby park. It houses a swing set and slide, all covered in graffiti and thick globs of shaving cream. Paula cannot stop staring at this image. The colours now dull, lifeless. They move into the line of trees separating the houses from the playground. The area under the trees are covered in dense undergrowth, twigs and leaves piercing Paula's exposed skin, adding to her ailments. She is sore and stiff and her head hurts. It smells too clean, too open out here. She longs for the smell of the city, for coffee shops and exhaust fumes and longs for noise. It is too quiet.

They stop in the middle of a clearing, Paula's feet heavy in the dirt. Twigs dangle from her shoelaces and scrape the undergrowth.

She squirms as if they are snakes, shaking them off. The woman is gone when she looks up.

A tree stands before her, gnarled, bent and hazel. It is the colour of her eyes. The colour of her nan's eyes. It is haloed in burgundy leaves which will soon drop. It reaches for her, murmuring soothing words, comfort, promising her love. When a branch moves towards her, Paula is hypnotised. She steps forwards, forgetting the pain, the loss, the pounding of her blood in her veins. Its touch is buttery soft against her skin. It traces her arm and clasps her hand, placing something inside before withdrawing into itself.

Paula looks at her palm and is surprised to recognise herself in the picture she finds, though she is only half-visible. It has been torn from one of her nan's scrapbooks. Beside her child self is her nan. Paula gasps. She forgot how young her nan looked, with her fire-engine red hair and unlined face, a wicked smile and kind, twinkling eyes like pools of melted chocolate. Paula cannot believe she is gone. She never said goodbye.

The branch reaches for her again. It grabs her wrist and pulls her attention towards it. The leaves she thought were ready to fall are flaming, dropping around her as embers. She stamps on some with her feet, hearing terrified shrieks, panics, tries to pull away but is held tighter. Paula frantically looks for the woman in black. She twists, head pounding, heart racing. The tree stands tall and welcomes her as an old friend. A door appears in its trunk, ringed in an orange glow and she is ushered inside, the branches pushing her as she tries to remain motionless, feet dug into the undergrowth. Her efforts are useless. It is cool inside, despite the raging inferno around her, and Paula is soothed by whispers.

Everything will be okay. A soft, familiar voice fills her head for a moment, gone before she can place it.

The door closes behind her, a draught blowing her hair up in raven tendrils which stick to her face. Paula swats them away, and when she sees the woman in black, eyes dancing in the flames, she forgets about everything else.

"What am I doing here?"

There is no response. Paula looks around. Sweat drips down her face, down her back, down her legs. Gross. She stands in a room no bigger than a broom cupboard or pantry, decorated in gold. It reminds her of her stuffy unit, though this is much nicer. Red rubies glitter at her, stuck in the grooves of the walls and floor. They whisper to her, asking her to touch them. She tucks her hands against her chest, cupping the picture to her heart. A droplet of blood from her grazed head falls towards the floor. It lands on a patch of gold and turns into a ruby with a little sizzle. Paula backs away, her hands pushing against the wall behind her, searching for an opening.

"You belong with me," the woman in black speaks, voice robotic. Cold. Distant. "You can never go home." The fire dances wickedly, leaving dark shadows on the face of the woman, making her skeletal.

To disguise her terror, Paula forces a laugh. The woman watches her, head tilted like an inquisitive dog. Paula finds an opening and pushes. Her fingers are through, sunlight is coming in. Fresh air. She needs to push harder. She keeps her face straight, hoping that it does not give her away, though her heart soars for a moment.

The woman in black sighs as if Paula has failed a test. Paula pulls her fingers back inside as her blood runs cold. A grin crosses the face of the woman in black as she unfurls her wings. Horrified, Paula bites her tongue to stop screaming, and blood fills her mouth. The woman's face elongates into that of a dragon, though her doll-like, static features are still evident underneath.

"You can never leave," the dragon-woman snarls. Fire tapers out of her nose and little beings spring to life from the walls. Winged eyeballs, nightmarish creatures coming for Paula. She opens her mouth to scream but it is trapped inside her so she falls to the floor, curls herself up against the gold wall and tries to wake up.

I must have hit my head hard on the gravel. Did I pass out?

Paula hears her nan. Though her eyes are shut and her skin shudders at the touch of the ghastly winged eyeball creatures, the woman from the picture materialises before her granddaughter. Paula wants to open her eyes, but she doesn't want her nan to leave again.

"My poor baby. You will be okay," she says, smoothing Paula's hair as she'd done so many times before. Nan puts her hand against Paula's face, staunching the bleeding. The pressure is nice, soothing.

"My dear, you are my Gothic Queen. This is a part of you. You need to absorb this side of yourself and face it. This is the only way for you to move on. I'm right here. I'm always with you."

Her nan fades away with these words, leaving Paula dazed on the floor, with little creatures buzzing around her like bees. She swats them away as she stands, keeping her eyes closed and uses the wall to guide her to the dragon-witch. There is a curious silence. Has she died?

Holding out her shaking left hand, Paula reaches towards what she hopes is a wing. Paula's hand strokes a leathery wing which twitches underneath her fingers. The silence is unending. Coolness swells. The trembling ground threatens to open up and swallow her. She holds on, imagining her nan holding on with her.

"It's okay, you belong with me," she whispers to the dragon-witch. Paula opens her eyes as the ground shakes violently, throwing her away from the dragon and into the wall, which opens up and spits Paula into the sunlight. She shields her eyes against the glare.

Paula stands facing the tree, but it is no longer burning. The leaves are not embers and there is no hint of smoke. The trees are still, the hazel one shrunken and shriveled to match the others. The tree she had been looking at is gone. There is no breeze, just a choking heat. Paula places her hand to her head. It is not bleeding. She looks around for a winged creature, a hint of gold, the woman in black. Nothing.

A piece of paper crinkles under her shoe. She picks it up. The edges are singed but Paula's nan smiles back at her from the photo. She stands in the clearing for a few more moments, waiting.

Goodbye, Nan.

She lets the picture fall to the undergrowth, kicking debris over it. The last thing she sees before she turns to leave are those hazel eyes, identical to her own.

* * *

Paula races to her bus terminal, dodging countless Hawaiian shirts and screaming children. Suitcases ram into her. People yell at her as she runs. She doesn't look back or say a thing. Her pocket holds the little fairy she found under the fridge. She liked the way the wings were bent like a dragon about to take flight and has a nagging memory surrounding this doll, but she can't quite place it. Paula is running out of time. Her bus will leave without her.

Paula reaches for the ticket, dislodging the fairy from her pocket. It tumbles to the ground, but Paula doesn't notice over the rumble of bus engines and the crowd. Paula does not see the crown carved into her forearm, glowing orange before fading to a black outline.

A little girl with midnight curls finds the discarded fairy. It looks like it has been trampled. The wings are crushed and covered in black glitter. The girl is delighted with her new toy. It is perfect.

"Come here my darling," her mother says. "You know you can't wander off. There are too many people here. I need to say goodbye. You be good for Nan. I will be home soon. Love you." The hurried and frantic tone of her mother makes the girl hide the fairy behind her back as she leans in to kiss her mother.

The young girl watches her mother board the bus, little hand tucked into a larger one. A she waves goodbye, a tear falls and traces a trail down her cheek. The little girl blows her a kiss, but her mother's back is turned and she misses it. The little girl imagines it lands on her mother's shoulder and stays with her.

After the bus pulls away, the girl squeezes her grandmother's hand. "Look Nan, I found this fairy. I want you to have her."

"Well, look at that. She is just darling. We will keep her safe, won't we, Paula?"

About the Author

Jordyn is a creative writer from the GunaiKurnai region in Victoria, Australia. She is a PhD student interested in disability advocacy and the myriad of ways to represent diverse lived experiences. With a passion for life writing and short fiction, Jordyn's work has appeared in *Kill Your Darlings, Tulpa Magazine, Mindshave* and the *Salty Tales Anthology*.

Make no mistake, the Capital City of New Zealand, Wellington, has got its fair share of ghouls and goblins.

THE GARAGE

Dane Divine

I bumped into her up at the Mount Vic Lookout. At first, I didn't recognise her.

"It's Kay," she stated, pulling back her wind-wrecked hair.

"Fuck, so it is," I said.

"Still swearing," she noted, rolling her eyes.

"Of course," I smiled, remembering some of the sweet little reasons we'd split up all those years before. Still, I want the world to be a place of peace and love, so to avoid being rude and just running away from her, I did the small-talk thing, feigning interest in her life whilst pointing out the landmarks of the city below. I was all about the "how nice to see you", "that's the harbour and over there is where the taniwha fell", "what are you doing here", "you see the tall buildings—that's the fault line", "how long are you staying", "yes, it's always windy but it's still the coolest little capital".

It turned out Kay was having a midlife crisis. Her beloved son had grown up and moved out of home as soon as he could, so she was on a solo trip to the other side of the planet to 'find herself'. After our breakup all those years ago, I'd moved to the other side of the planet to live a happy life, so unfortunately she had also found me.

"You're here alone?" I asked.

"Yes," she said. "Being on one's own builds character." Adding, "It's so good to see you." She grabbed my arm. "I haven't spoken to anyone in days. Let's go for dinner."

"But I was on my way home from work," I explained. "I just came up here for some fresh air."

She gave me a sad look that at one time would have sucked me in, but now it just seemed like she had something wrong with her lips.

"I'm not dressed for dinner. I'd have to go home and change," I said, planning on driving home and hiding there until she'd left the country. "We could meet later? Maybe next week?"

She smiled with a mad desperate look in her eyes. "I walked up and I'm free. I can come with you right now. I don't mind waiting for you to change. It'll be fun."

And that's how I ended up driving home on a Thursday evening with my long and happily forsaken ex, Kay. It was nice to see her in a way, every time she opened her mouth, it reminded me why separating was the best thing we'd ever done.

From the Lookout, I drove down an evening sun-dappled Alexandra Road towards Newtown. By the time we'd reached the Zoo, Kay had criticized my driving, the narrow roads and steep hills of Wellington, the driving ability of everyone we'd passed, New Zealand architecture, the pedestrians, New Zealand fashion sense, and everything else she could see. Negativity oozed out of her like slime oozes from a dead slug.

As I drove up the curvy hill to my place, I made a plan: I'd park on my street and leave her waiting in the car while I slipped away down the steps beside my garage. That way Kay wouldn't be able to guess which was my house and I could protect myself from any future unexpected visits. I'd change , run back up the stairs and we'd drive into town. Kay was staying at the backpackers so I'd park on Kent Terrace, walk down to Courtenay Place and eat at Sweet Mother's Kitchen or get some tapas at Basque. After kai and some polite kōrero, I would drive home and avoid her for the rest of my life. Yet sometimes, things do not go to plan. My street was way too busy to park on, so I had to use my garage, which had my house number on it. I sighed.

"Still sighing," she said.

I rolled my eyes, reminding myself this would soon be over.

My garage is a double garage. It's perched on stilts on the road above my basement flat, which, like most of Welly's housing, is nestled lower down on the hillside. I share the garage space with my upstairs neighbours. Mine's the door on the right. There's a space for my car and I've stacked my camping gear and bikes down the far end.

My neighbours have their own roller-door too, but I don't know how they'll ever get anything else in their half, because their side is a hoarder's dream. The biggest item is an old, white car. By the looks of its square lines, it's from the early 80s. The windows appear tinted, although it's hard to tell because everything's covered in a thick, nasty, yellowish dust. There's other stuff too: an old bookcase; a bag full of those little white polystyrene beads that go inside beanbags; lots of packing boxes full of useless junk; various pieces of broken furniture; an old mirror that doesn't reflect much apart from weirdly-shaped shadows; and countless other random items. I've had a glance, but it's their stuff, so I leave it alone.

Kay, however, is the nosiest fucker I've ever met. Even before opening the garage door, I knew her being there was a bad idea.

Pressing the remote control, the electronic roller-door curled upwards. I drove forward and headed in, a manoeuvre I've made hundreds of times, despite the row of cars parked on the opposite side of the narrow road allowing minimal turning space. But as I turned, Kay piped up.

"Careful," she said. "Move a little to the left. The other left. Yes, the right. Stop. Stop. Be gentle. No, more gentle. Now just ease it in like I direct. Now, hard, turn hard." She reached over and pulled at the steering wheel, reminding me of another reason we'd not survived as a loving couple.

Despite her kind assistance, I parked the car without a scratch. Once I'd stopped, Kay got out and walked straight over to my neighbour's dusty vehicle.

"Look, a car," she exclaimed, as if I hadn't noticed it before.

I sighed, exasperated, as she peered in at the windows.

"Is it yours?"

"It's my neighbours. I don't touch their stuff," I hinted. "Do you want to wait in the car? I'll only be a minute."

Kay ignored me, took a tissue out of her bag, spat on it and rubbed a small patch clean.

"Kay, please," I sighed, "they'll notice."

"Oh worry-puss," she laughed, waving an arm in my direction, "they obviously never come in here."

At that moment Miss Fluffypants turned up. She's nosey too, but in a different way. Being a bit psychopathic, she likes to assess any changes to see if there's anything she can kill, although she's a darling cat, really. Normally she avoids the garage, for some strange reason, but she must have heard me talking so had come up to see what was happening.

"Kay," I called, happy for the distraction, "come and meet my cat."

I leant down to pick up Miss Fluffypants, Kay pulled on the car's mucky door handle. I rose and turned, the cat now in my arms, and to all of our surprise the door clicked open. It was unlocked.

I took a step back.

"Eughhh, it smells bad," Kay said, flapping her fingers under her nose.

"Come away from there," I whined.

But Kay moved in closer, pulling the door open wider.

I opened my mouth to tell Kay to shut the door and stop nosing, when Miss Fluffypants struggled in my arms. She's never scratched me, ever, but this time she dug her claws in so hard that I yelped and let her go. As she jumped, I swear to God, these enormous, thin, brown, legs stretched out from inside the car.

In that moment, my instincts kicked in and I attempted to combat the creature with a sonic attack, well, I screamed. Kay stood frozen in horror. One moment the dark legs were reaching out to encircle her shoulders, the next she was dragged into the opening and had disappeared into the car. The door closed with a soft click.

Stunned by the sudden peace, quiet and empty space, I stood staring at the car. Then I thought maybe Kay was trying to mess with my head. After all, she'd always been good at that.

"Kay," I hissed softly, so the monster wouldn't hear me, "you can come out now." But there was no answer. I considered going over to look inside or calling my neighbours for help, but how could I explain someone had been poking around their car, or worse, what if they knew what was in there? I figured the AA wouldn't be able to help, as it wasn't my car or technically a mechanical problem, so I called the police.

* * *

"Since the incident you've been waiting here, outside the garage?" one of the police officers asked.

"Yes."

"And when was this?"

I checked my phone. "I called at six twenty-three." I said, showing her my out-going call display.

"And you say she went into the car and hasn't come out?"

"She was dragged in, by something with scary legs."

"Well, I'll just go and have a look," she said, raising her eyebrows in disbelief.

Being sensible I took some steps back. The other officer did too. I thought about saying, 'Don't go,' but if she got eaten by the car-thing too, at least this time there would be a witness.

From a safe distance on the road outside the garage, we watched as she walked into the gloom towards the car. She looked the car up and down, under, over and around. "Very dirty," she noted, peering through the clean patch on the windscreen. "Nothing visible in there." Then she touched the door handle.

The other police officer and I both took a deep breath and held it.

"Please, don't," I warned. But she looked back at us with a patronising smile and opened the door.

Again, the legs appeared and sucked her into the car. Again, the door shut with a gentle click.

"Fucking hell," the other police officer said.

I shook my head. "Yeah, nah," I said, in a told you so kind of way.

* * *

After a few more personnel losses, the police called in the rego. It turned out nobody owned the car. My neighbours said it had been there since they moved in and they assumed it belonged to our landlord. The landlord thought it was theirs. The police decided to remove the car. Finally I'd be able to use the garage and my car again. Nothing was mentioned of Kay. But before the police truck arrived to tow it away, the dusty old car mysteriously disappeared, leaving an empty space and some stains on the wooden garage floor. So, if you ever see an abandoned white Toyota Camry on the side of the road, best leave it alone.

About the Author:

Dane Divine (she/her) is an author of speculative fiction. Her work has been published in Retreat West's *The Word for Freedom, The Moon Magazine*, and in the 2021 Wellington Zinefest publication: *Coven*. Dane was one of the winners in a *Shoreline of Infinity* sci-fi micro-fiction competition, and was top ten short-listed for one of their short story competitions.

Born in Plymouth, on the South West coast of the UK, Dane now lives in Wellington, on the South West coast of the North Island of New Zealand (Te Wanganui-a-Tara, Te Ika-a-Māui, Aotearoa). Dane describes herself as a 'queer, dyke, sapphic, witch, author'. She writes about magic, sex, fear, obsession, and nasty little murderous tantrums. When she's not writing or reading, you'll find her outdoors, either on her mountain bike or in the garden.

Find out more at:
danedivine.com, www.facebook.com/danedivinestories, instagram.com/dane_divine

ABOUT DEADSET PRESS

Deadset Press is an independent publisher of incredible speculative fiction. We provide publishing pathways for emerging writers from Australia and New Zealand, and aspire to shine the light on unique and diverse voices.

You can learn more at:

www.deadsetpress.com

ALSO BY DEADSET PRESS

Charity Anthologies

Stories of Hope

Stories of Survival

The Zodiac Series

Capricorn (The Zodiac Series #1)

Aquarius (The Zodiac Series #2)

Pisces (The Zodiac Series #3)

Aries (The Zodiac Series #4)

Taurus (The Zodiac Series #5)

Gemini (The Zodiac Series #6)

Cancer (The Zodiac Series #7)

Leo (The Zodiac Series #8)

Virgo (The Zodiac Series #9)

Libra (The Zodiac Series #10)

Scorpio (The Zodiac Series #11)

Sagittarius (The Zodiac Series #12)